REPENTANCE

Westerman Tales

WILLIAM BURGDORF

BOOKS BY
WILLIAM BURGDORF

Westerman Tales

Red River Station
Repentance

The Bierman Saga

The New Mexican

Company A

The Arizonan

Humps and Hooves

BOOKS BY
WILLIAM BURGDORF

Westerman Tales

Red River Station
Repentance

The Bierman Saga

The New Mexican

Company A

The Arizonan

Humps and Hooves

DEDICATION

I've dedicated this book to the two hundred Deputy U.S. Marshals who served Judge Isaac Parker's court of the U.S. Western District of Arkansas from 1875 until 1896.

This group of men covered 74,000 square miles of Indian Territory with authority to make arrests with or without warrant for: murder, manslaughter, assault with intent to kill or to maim, attempt to murder, arson, robbery, rape, bribery, burglary, larceny, incest, or adultery.

Sixty-nine Deputies were killed in the line of duty.

And to Nancy, who carries her own badge and speaks with authority.

1

STRUNG UP

THE HOT TEXAS SUN BEATS DOWN ON THE SKINNY, BIB overalled farmer as he stops, reaches in his back pocket, and pulls out a red bandana. He shakes it open and wipes the sweat from his brow, then his head.

I've stretched that barbed wire at least a hundred yards.

Dug every dadburn post hole and set them poles.

Rolled out the wire.

I'm going to protect my crops and keep cattle from crashing through this year.

A metallic clipping sound behind him causes him to look over his shoulder.

"What do you think you're doing?" He shouts at a cowboy wearing a dirty grey sweat stained slouch cavalry hat with tarnished gold tassels and a long black duster sitting on his horse with wire cutters in his hand.

A single strand of the three rows of barbed wire is still attached to a post the farmer placed earlier.

The pistol in the hand of a second cowboy wearing a sombrero with his serape flung back over his right shoulder motions the farmer closer to the fence.

The farmer moves beside the wire.

Leaning over in the saddle, the cowboy in the duster clips the last wire. The barbed wire quickly recoils in a serpentine-like motion seeking to return to its original bundle shape.

As the wire wraps around him, the farmer lets out a scream. He stands firm momentarily, then his foot slips, and he rolls up into the bundle shouting, shrieking, and cursing. The barbs shred his clothes and skin. Blood begins flowing and stains the dry ground as the farmer is twisted into the coiling cloak of pain. The wire gouges and slices deeper into his body as the devil's necklace constricts tighter and tighter.

The cowboy drops the wire cutter into his saddlebag as both ride away. Their cattle are bunched up, waiting over the hill.

Chadbourne Westerman adjusts the collar of his white shirt, tugs at his vest, and uses his fork to corral the last apple pie crumbs on his plate. He sits at the window table in Mollie Love's Restaurant in Red River Station. Across the table, Isaac Wisenheimer shakes the newspaper he holds in front of him to turn a page. His dove gray suit doesn't look like it has a wrinkle.

"I don't know why you had to take the Deputy U.S. Marshal

job anyway. We were doing just fine moving from ranch to ranch helping solve rustling, land grabbing, and sundry problems for our clients."

"When Mr. McCray talked to me about this job, I couldn't turn him down."

"You mean when Senator McCray approached you, and I know that we tracked the person who killed his son." Isaac pauses remembering the cattle drive on the Chisholm Trail. *Cowboys killed indiscriminately by a crazed killer that stalked the drive. Chadbourne and I confounded by suspects and situations until the incident in Abilene that required me to shoot my love, Abigail. I still fail to understand the depth of grief and revenge that drive people to such extreme actions.*

"Yep. MCray did take that senator job in Austin and was kind enough to remember and entertain us for dinner when we passed through. He introduced us to that Federal Judge."

"Of course, you needed to bring up the fact that you were looking for something more stable than range detective, and he sort of mentioned the judge needing a Deputy U.S. Marshal in north Texas."

"Yep, sure is real curious how that happened."

"Oh yes, it *certainly* is curious. So, here we are."

"What are you complaining about. You've always liked Mollie's place."

"Oh, I like it here all right, especially since most the dirty, noisy herds have drifted west of here for crossing the Red River."

"I understand Dodge City, Kansas, is as bad as Abilene used to be."

"It's an end-of-the-trail-town. It is bound to be troublesome when herds arrive. Do you intend to go back up the trail, the Western Trail?"

"Nope. Done all the drivin' I hanker to do. I'm set with keepin' an eye on north Texas and the Territory."

"Well, it's your job. Besides, I'm just along for the adventure." Isaac sits back and laughs aloud. "Yes, the adventure. That's what I am seeking."

Chad motions the waiter for more coffee and watches as his cup is filled.

It's been a few years since Abilene and the trail drive. Manolito, our Mexican cook, Isaac, and I came back down the Chisholm Trail and picked up the drover's new boots from Justin's in Red River Station. We delivered them to the boys in San Antonio. Then, we busted around central Texas investigating cattle problems for a few years. When I met up with the senator in Austin, I took him up on being a deputy marshal. It's a good life.

The front door of Mollie's flings open, capturing Chad's attention. A barefoot boy in dirty Levis held up with suspenders bursts into the dining room. Pausing, he looks around, and runs to Chad.

"Marshal come quick. Some ranch hands brought a sodbuster to the doctor."

"So, what's that got to do with me?"

"He was rolled up in barbed wire and mumblin' somethin' about cowboys cutting his fence."

Yanking his suit jacket from the back of his chair, Chad rises, kicks the furniture back, and rushes after the boy through the open door. Isaac throws down his newspaper and hurries out right behind them.

Chad watches the town's doctor as he works on the man stretched out on the table. Doctor Sidney Baker moves rapidly, checking the farmer's pulse, staunching blood flow, and tries to keep his patient alive. He is short, wears a brown three-piece suit, and a white shirt. His suit coat is thrown over a nearby chair, and his shirt sleeves are rolled up to his elbows. The office is small and has one examination table with a large kerosene lamp suspended above it. In the corner is a desk beside a bookshelf that overflows with textbooks. A potbelly stove sits in the middle of the room, and four chairs are scattered around. Against the wall, beside the table, sits a cupboard with opened doors. Bottles, beakers, bandages, pans, and medical instruments litter the shelves.

"Are you gonna be able to save him, Sidney?" asks Chad.

Isaac sits in a chair beside the desk.

"Don't know, Chad. He's lost a lot of blood."

"Isaac, come take a look."

"No, thank you. Sanguineous drainage and I don't agree." Blood from the body continues to pool on the table and drip incessantly to the floor. Isaac glances away.

"That's it." Sidney straightens up.

"What's it?" Chad stares at the doctor.

"Gone."

"Gone, like dead?"

"I've lost him, Chad."

"I thought you doctors can heal anything."

"Don't be so naïve. Doctors aren't miracle workers. His blood loss was too much to overcome."

"So, he bled to death?"

"That's what I'm writing on the certificate. Death by exsanguination."

"How can I find out who did this with him dead?"

"Not my problem, Marshal. My job's done. You better get after yours. I hope you have better luck than I did." The doctor walks to the water basin at the end of the examination table and washes his hands and arms. He dries them on a towel and rolls his sleeves down to his wrists. He picks up his coat and puts it on.

"I'm goin' to the saloon for a drink. Care to join me?" Doctor Baker looks at Chad and Isaac.

"You just gonna leave him lying there?" Chad glances down at the bloody man on the table.

"He doesn't feel a thing now, lying there or anywhere else. I'll let the mortician know to pick up the body." The doctor walks to the office door, opens it, and leaves.

Isaac is right behind him.

Chad walks over and touches the corpse. "I'll find whoever did this to you, friend. It ain't right to have to leave this life like you did. I'll find 'em."

He follows Doc Baker and Isaac to the saloon.

2

OLD HABITS

THE AFTERNOON SUN POUNDS DOWN ON THE SMALL herd of thirty cattle plodding along the well-worn trail leading toward the Red River. The treeless landscape is wave after wave of rolling hills, scattered brush, and grass belly-deep to their horses.

"What are we gonna do with these beeves." The sombrero wearing cowboy flips the end of his lariat smacking the rear-end of a slow-moving cow. He wears a brown leather vest and canvas pants. His face displays a large handlebar moustache with waxed upturned tips.

"We're crossin' the Red River near Doan's adobe house. There's a solid bottom shallow ford." Rafe Dolin removes his dirty cavalry hat and slaps it against his chaps. His long greasy black hair hangs to his shoulders. Slapping the hat against the chest of his duster to knock loose trail dirt, he resets it back on his head. He runs a hand over the stubble of his unshaved face.

"Yeah. So, what then?"

"We'll push these critters into Indian Territory."

"So you got buyers waitin' for you?"

"We'll see."

"Listen, Rafe. I ain't about to babysit no cows. I went along with your rustlin' a few head to sell, quick like."

"Victor, you're free to cut lose any time you feel like it."

"Just because you keep tryin' to steal cattle from the drives don't mean that's for me."

"Any time you're feelin' froggy, just jump, *amigo*." Rafe's hand slides toward his pistol. He wears it on the opposite side of his body from his dominant right hand. The holster is tilted forward to allow for a quick cross-body draw. His weathered duster is pulled back to keep it out of the way. From under the brim of his dirty gray Fort Knox cavalry hat he watches his partner's movements.

Victor slowly moves both hands away from his waist and scratches his beard stubble.

"It's okay, *amigo*. We'll take the cattle across the river at Doan's and into the Territory. Maybe, we can sell them there. *Si*?"

Rafe relaxes. With his right hand he wipes his wispy black moustache and smiles. "Good to see we have an understandin', amigo. Keep pushin' the cattle. I'd like to be across the river tonight just in case we have anybody trailin' us."

"*Si. Si, compadre.* You tied up that farmer, no? He will only squeal from the wire for a little while, *si*?"

"I hate that damned barbed wire. I'm seein' it more and

more up Kansas way and comin' over from Arkansas too. Damned sodbusters are plowin' up the open range and now they're stringin' that damn devil's necklace over every foot of empty prairie."

"Maybe it is something you cannot stop, no?"

"Oh, I'll stop it every time I come across it, and I'll stop 'em when I see 'em. Now, *vamonos*, let's get to Doan's."

"*Si, amigo*. We go." Victor spurs toward straying cattle pushing them forward.

The small clapboard room seems confining. The back wall has a steel barred cell sitting in the corner and a desk on the opposite side of the room. On the wall behind the desk hangs a rifle rack with a shotgun and two Henry repeaters. A small stove in the middle of the room has a coffeepot sitting on it. Chadbourne sits in one of the four straight backed chairs, Isaac in another, a small barefoot boy in the third, and his father in the fourth.

"Tell 'em again what you saw, Sammy," says the father. He brushes dirt from the leg of his overalls, rerolls his flannel shirt sleeve, and tucks his scuffed, worn, brogan shoes under the chair.

"I already told 'em I saw two cowboys. A skinny one in a black duster, and the other'en was a Mex wearin' a sombrero and serape."

"You were comin' up from the creek bottom and saw the cowboy cut the wire that wrapped up the farmer, right?" Chad leans closer.

"Yes, sir. He cut the wire, laughed, and then they rode off leavin' Mr. Jones screamin', cryin', and bleedin' bad like."

"What did you do then?"

"Ran fast as I could to get Pap."

"He did do that, Marshal. I come on the run, found Jones all wrapped up, and tried to talk to him. Weren't no good. He mumbled about cowboys cuttin' wire. I fetched my buckboard and got him to town fast as I could. That's the gospel truth."

"I don't doubt you. Can you tell me anymore about the cowboy?"

"Tell him, Sammy. Tell him everything."

"He was skinny, had a mousy moustache, was squinty-eyed, wore his pistol tilted close to his belt buckle, and wore a dirty black duster. He had an old cavalry hat with tassels on his head. That's all I remember seein'."

"Thank you, son. I appreciate all you've told me. Y'all are free to go."

The father and son quickly leave, and Isaac moves to a seat beside Chad.

"You have some idea about this, don't you?"

"I got a gut-feelin', that's all."

"What does it tell you?"

"I'm thinkin' I've crossed paths with that cowboy before."

"Where?"

"Do you remember on the drive to Abilene when I went out and found that gang followin' the herd?"

"Yes. You came back and said four men were following and might try to do something to rustle cattle. Nothing ever happened."

"I hid out and watched the four men at their campfire. Got a good look at them."

"So, the description of this cowboy fits one of them?"

"I'm thinkin' it does. Do you recall when we found the two dead men by the Arkansas River?"

"One snake bitten and the other crushed. Were they two of the four?"

"Yep. I don't recall any Mex with them, but the black duster and hat with tassels triggered my memory."

"We've chased down a number of malcontents and law breakers in the past few years. There are plenty of men with dusters and tasseled hats. It does not mean this one is the one you saw on the Chisholm Trail."

"You're right as rain, Isaac. My gut says otherwise, and I think I'll go with it."

"All right, Marshal, we go with your gut to where?"

"I'm going to get word out to ranchers and farmers around here about any missing livestock. If this is the man I'm thinkin' it is, he hasn't changed his ways. He's still a rustler."

Standing, Chad leads Isaac out of the building, heading for the saloon to start spreading word about the threat of rustling.

It's been two days of impatiently waiting. Chad's maintained a vigil at the saloon, listening for any talk of rustled cattle. The batwing doors swing inward as Isaac walks into the cool dimness of the saloon. He pauses to let his eyes adjust after leaving the bright sunlight. Chad waves from a table in the middle of the room.

"How long are you going to camp out here?" Isaac walks to

Chad's table, pulls out a chair, and sits down.

"Oh, I reckon for about as long as it takes. Hopefully, not much longer." Chad nods at two cowboys approaching his table. The taller of the two walks toward Chad.

"I hear you're askin' around about rustled cattle. Is that right?" He pushes his hat back on his head and straightens his denim shirt.

"Could be. What do you know?"

"I know that we have about thirty to forty head missing from the south pasture." The cowboy props one foot up on the seat of the chair across from Chad. He leans in. "Hard to get an exact count, but it appears they been gone for about a week."

"Where you boys from?"

"Max Fuller's spread west of town. Max said to look you up."

"You got a line camp watchin' over your livestock?"

"Nope. We ride out every now and then to check the stock. Been a few days gettin' to the south pasture. Noticed the smaller numbers right away."

"You find any trail?"

"Followed some tracks for a ways headin' northwest. Lost them in creek crossin's and hard rock country."

"I'm obliged. Have a beer on me." Chad signals the barkeep to set up beers for the cowboys. He motions to Isaac. "Pay the bartender, I'm headin' for the livery to get our horses and will pick up some supplies as well. Meet me there in an hour." Chad walks out of the saloon.

Isaac shoves his chair back, walks to the bar, lays four bits on the counter, nods to the cowboys, and pushes through the batwing doors. He pauses on the porch.

Yes, sir. Just like that we're off again. What did I say at Maggie's about hanging around with Chadbourne? Oh, yes. I'm just in it for the adventure. Yes. The adventure.

He walks toward the boarding house to pack clothing, shaving items, and personal effects in saddlebags before joining Chad.

3

LEGALITY

A COLD WIND BLOWS OUT OF THE NORTH AND WHIPS around the corners of the brick two-story building sitting on the bluff overlooking the Arkansas River. The man standing at the second-floor window listens to the howling wind. His hands are clasped behind his back. He wears a three-piece black suit and has wavy brown hair, a moustache, and chin whiskers. The only sound in the office is the steady ticking from the swinging pendulum of the large wall clock. A desk sits in the middle of the room covered in papers. A high-backed chair behind it is positioned to look out of three large windows. There's a six-man gallows in the yard below. A spittoon sits in front of the desk between two straight-backed arm chairs. The door opens as a clerk enters.

"Your Honor."

"What is it Blakely?"

"You'll need to review the docket before court."

"Very well, sit it on my desk."

"Sir, if you'll look at it now, I'll post it right away."

"Blakely, President Ulysses S. Grant appointed me U.S. District Judge for the Western District of Arkansas, knowing how opposed to the death penalty I am. Did you know that?" The man at the window turns around to face the clerk.

"No, sir. I didn't."

"Now, I have Arkansas and the Indian Territory to adjudicate and some of the worst vermin imaginable to deal with. People are calling me the 'Hanging Judge'. Me, Isaac Parker. Have you heard them?"

"Well, they don't understand, Your Honor."

"Have you heard them?"

"I, uh, well, yes. I have."

"Give me that docket." Snatching the paper from the clerk's hand he quickly reviews it and hands it back. "Move item one to the third spot. Post the docket. Make the attorneys happy."

"Thank you, Judge Parker. I'll post it at once."

"Send in that Texas marshal. What's his name?"

"Chadbourne Westerman, Your Honor. You telegraphed him two weeks ago to come to Fort Smith and meet with you."

"Yes, yes, I remember. Do you think I'm forgetful?"

"Oh, no, Your Honor."

"Well, get out of here and send him in immediately."

"There's a problem, sir. He's here, in Fort Smith, but left when you didn't see him right away. I'll send someone to find him."

"Damn-nation, find him and get him in here now. Move. Go get him."

"Yes, Your Honor. Going now, Your Honor." The clerk rushes from the office, carefully closing the door behind him.

How in the hell can I adjudicate this district? My marshals are spread so thin it's a wonder they can apprehend anyone, let alone transport them to Fort Smith for trial. The Territory seems to overflow with outlaws and low life scum, white, Indian, and Mexican. Arkansas is not much better. They waylay, bushwhack, and ambush my marshals daily. It's a wonder any are alive. Now, I have eastern and southern Kansas farmers petitioning the court for protection against fence cutting. Farmers in Arkansas and the Territory are jumping on the wagon. Hell, fence cutting is the lowest priority on my totem pole, but the farmers keep yelling all the way to Washington. This Texas marshal better give me some support. I don't have any more men to spare.

The hotel four buildings down the block from the courthouse is busy in the mornings. Chad sits in the lobby in an overstuffed Queen Anne chair watching the patrons descend from second and third floor sleeping rooms. The sweeping stairway is busier than many roadways he's seen in Texas. The stately brick hotel has a generous lobby with potted plants in the corners, brocade covered stuffed chairs and couches arranged around the room, a large carved walnut reception desk, and gas lit wall lamps with a large suspended chandelier. He watches a short, balding man in pinstriped trousers, white shirt with garters on his sleeves rush into the hotel and up to the front desk. He has a frantic discussion with the hotel clerk who points Chad's direction.

"Marshal Westerman? You are Marshal Westerman, aren't you?" The man stands fidgeting in front of Chad.

Chad lowers the paper he's been reading. "Who wants to know?"

"Marshal, I've been sent by Judge Parker's office to collect you. His Honor would like to meet with you, right away." The man gestures toward the hotel door.

Chad slowly folds his paper and lays it on the sofa. "It's right nice of His Honor to want to see me since I've been camped out here for almost a week waiting on him. Might be I'll wander over to the office later to see if he's real busy or not."

"Please, sir don't make this any more difficult than it already is. I'm just an assistant clerk, but I've been tasked to collect you and bring you to the office now."

"Friend, you're in an unenviable position. You might say between a rock and a hard place. However, I don't want to see your standing in the Judge's office jeopardized, so lead the way, my good man. Let's go visit the Judge." Chad stands and slowly saunters out of the hotel as the clerk races toward the courthouse.

The clerk raps on the tall wooden door to Judge Parker's office. Rushing around the office six clerks deliver file folders and papers among the four desks in the room.

"Enter." A deep baritone voice responds from behind the door. The court clerk eases open the door and steps inside.

"Marshal Westerman is here, Your Honor."

"Well, let him in. Stop blocking the doorway, Blakely. Let the man come in."

"Yes, Your Honor."

The clerk steps out of the way and holds the door open for Chadbourne.

"You can go in, Marshal."

"Thank you, Blakely. Sounds like the 'he bull' is in rare form today." Chad smiles and Blakely smirks at his comment.

Chad walks into Judge Parker's office, pauses to look around, and moves toward a chair in front of the large cluttered desk. Parker watches his approach, stands, moves around the desk, and extends his right hand.

"Glad you're here, Marshal. It's about time we met."

Chad grasps the extended hand and they share a firm handshake.

"Sit down, Marshal. Take a seat." Parker moves back around his desk to sit in the leather-covered swivel chair. Chad sits in one of the leather Queen Anne chairs.

"I've been camped out in Fort Smith for a while, Judge, waitin' on you. Was fixin' to leave for Texas today or tomorrow." Chad removes his Stetson and tosses it onto the seat beside him.

"That would have been a real mistake, Marshal. I'd have probably considered that 'in contempt' and sent marshals to arrest you."

"You are a real ripsnorter ain't you, Judge."

Parker smiles.

"My good man, you've not seen anything, yet."

"I hear they are callin' you the 'Hanging Judge', and your jail is called 'Hell on the Border.'"

The smile vanishes from Parker's face.

"Let's be very clear, Marshal. I never hanged a man. It is the law."

"Okay. I can understand that. What do you want with me?"

"It seems we've gotten off on the wrong foot. I'm sorry for the delay in meeting with you. The court requires attention, my marshals need information and directions, and most days are not my own. I'm not defending being discourteous, simply sharing what the circumstances are."

"Judge, I suppose that I'm a pragmatist too. Many times, things just are what they are. Ain't no other way to explain it."

Parker leans forward and places his arms on the desk.

"You know, Marshal. There may be hope for both of us yet. You've shared what you've heard about me, let me say that a mutual friend, Senator McCray of the Texas Legislature, says you are a trustworthy man."

"I appreciate the kind words from the Senator. I've worked for him in the past, and we seem to 'gee and haw' just fine."

With a loud laugh, Parker sits back reclining in his chair.

"'Gee and haw.' Now, that's a good one. Knowing when to turn left or right as a team is mighty important. Do you think that we can reach a point of being able to 'gee and haw' together?"

"I reckon I'm up for it, Your Honor. Don't see why we can't try."

A sharp rapping on the chamber door interrupts the conversation. Blakely eases the door open and sticks his head into the office.

"Your Honor, court is preparing to begin. You'll be needed shortly."

"Get out of here, Blakely, and shut the door. Court begins

when I say it begins. The accused and their attorneys can cool their heels a while longer." Parker bellows.

Blakely shuts the door with a pop.

"Sorry for the interruption, Marshal. We were just beginning to get acquainted. Tell me a little about Chadbourne Westerman." Parker reclines in his chair and clasps his hands together over his stomach.

"Your Honor, ain't too much to tell. I'm a Texan. Pa moved us from San Antonio to Uvalde in '60 to raise horses. He served in the Frontier Battalion during the war keeping the Indians at bay. In '64, I was old enough to join the Confederate army just in time for the last battle at Palmito Ranch near Brownsville, Texas. I was part of Colonel Giddings cavalry. We whipped the Yankees real good. Sent them runnin' seven miles to Brazos Island. In the next couple of days, General Slaughter and Colonel Ford came to say we'd surrendered and lost the war. A bunch of us boys took off for home right away instead of becoming prisoners of war."

"Yes, I remember reading all the newspaper accounts of the battle. You all fought after Robert E. Lee had surrendered, but Kirby Smith wasn't ready to quit."

"I got home to Uvalde and raised horses with Pa. In '66, we drove a herd to San Antonio to sell to the Yankee occupation army. When we got back home, Apaches had attacked the ranch, killed Ma and my brothers and sisters. It crushed Pa. He was never the same."

"Sorry to hear that, Marshal."

"It was what it was, Judge. Pa sent me up the Chisholm Trail in '67. We rounded up some loose cattle to add to a herd that was formin' up for a drive to Abilene. He died while I was away. When I returned to Texas, I met Mister McCray and worked as his top hand. In '71, McCray sent me on the trail of a killer that hanged his only boy. I became a range detective, caught the killer in Abilene, and settled the score. I bounced around after that solving range cases until Senator McCray asked me to become a U.S. Marshal. That's my story."

"You've led some life, Marshal. I'm about to ask you to add additional chapters to your story, if you've a mind to."

"I don't know how much more I can talk, Judge. I'm gettin' mighty parched and needin' somethin' to whet my whistle. Can we adjourn to a saloon?"

"Marshal, if I try to leave this room, I'll never make it through the door. Those clerks out there are lined up three deep with affidavits, summons, parole requests, and certificates I ain't yet heard about. No, we're better off right here."

Parker reaches for a bottom desk drawer, opens it, and pulls out a half-full bottle of Old Grand Dad. He sits two glasses on the desk and splashes whiskey into both of them. He scoots a glass to Chad, corks and puts the bottle back in the drawer, and picks up his glass.

"Here's mud in your eye, Marshal." Parker tosses the drink into his mouth and swallows. With a slight cough, he says, "Mighty fine, Marshal. Give it a go."

Chad tosses down his drink as well and sits the empty glass on the desk.

"Just what we needed, Judge. Now, what do you want me to do?"

The late morning sun beats through the three windows in Judge Parker's chambers. Chad sits in the Queen Anne chair, his elbows propped on the arms, his hands clasped together, and his fingers steepled under his chin. Parker reclines in his swivel chair with his hands clasped across his stomach.

"So, If I understand correctly, all you want me to do is end the wire cutting in the eastern part of Indian Territory, and in southern and eastern Kansas." Chad glances out the window at the gallows. "You think it's bein' done by a Texas outlaw named Rafe Dolin. This man is a known rustler, murderer, rapist, and a man burner. He preys on farmers and homesteads and may ride with a Mexican partner. Is that about it?"

"That sums it up nicely. We believe the Mexican is named Victor or Victorio Gonzales."

"Uh huh, and why don't your other U.S. Marshals take care of the problem?"

"Everybody is strapped, and all my marshals are spread too thin already. I've had to call in reinforcements. That's you."

"I have a partner. Would you deputize him as well?"

"If you vouch for him, I'll swear him in, too."

"Because I need to make a livin', how much does this job pay?"

"I'll compensate you the same as my other marshals. You'll receive two dollars for making an arrest and up to six cents a mile going out, and ten cents a mile for returning a prisoner to this court. Most of my marshals earn around five hundred dollars a year. You can turn in receipts for reimbursement of expenses like ammunition, food, and necessary supplies."

"Sounds like you've got this all figured out."

"I wouldn't be the Hanging Judge if I didn't." Parker smiles.

"I reckon that's right, Your Honor. When do I start?"

"You were already on the job when you arrived in Fort Smith. Now, get out of my chambers. I have a full day of court issues to deal with and you're taking my valuable time."

Chad stands, picks up his hat, and walks toward the door.

"You want Rafe Dolin alive or dead, Your Honor?" Chad pauses with his hand on the doorknob, waiting for the Judge's reply.

"I want justice served, Marshal. A court of law will determine his sentence. I don't want him to escape and continue his bloody rampage. Serve him justice. Get to it."

"Yes, Your Honor." Chad opens the door, leaves the office, and slowly walks down the hallway.

Isaac ain't gonna believe what we're fixin' to tie into. I may have just hitched us to a cyclone. This has to be the outlaw I missed dealin' with on the Chisholm Trail. Don't know how Isaac's gonna cotton to bein' a Deputy U.S. Marshal.

4

DEPUTIZED

THE DINING ROOM OF THE HOTEL IS BRIGHTLY LIT with three large chandeliers. The dozen tables are arranged in a staggered manner. Each table has four straight-backed padded chairs. The back wall has two doorways that waiters move through to access the kitchen. A sideboard along the wall of the lobby holds glasses, dishes, and pitchers sweating water off their exteriors. Seated at a table in the corner beside the front window, Isaac leans over to talk with Chad.

"Why, why in a thousand years would I ever be deputized?"

"Got me, partner."

"I could not, would not, should not…ever."

"Yep."

"What did you do to help me?"

"Vouched for you."

"Thanks. Thanks a lot."

"You're welcome. What else are friends for?"

"Friends. That what you call us?"

"Yep."

"Would a friend stand beside someone and let them make a horrendous mistake?"

"Depends."

"What? What do you mean…depends?"

"Well, if the one friend needed the other friend to help them do somethin' that the one friend might not want to do, then the one friend would make sure to stand beside the other friend to do it."

"What? Do you ever listen to yourself? Sometimes you talk, and the words just keep stumbling out of your mouth."

"Nope."

"I stood there in Judge Parker's office and let him swear me in as a Deputy U.S. Marshal and you just stood there smiling… smiling."

"Yep."

"What if I don't do this?"

"I imagine Parker will say you're in contempt of the court and hang you."

"Oh, you are funny, real funny, Westerman."

"Yep."

"What are we supposed to do? My mind went blank when I raised my hand to take the oath. I don't remember what the Judge said about our assignment."

"Real simple. Find Rafe Dolin. Stop him. Bring him back to Fort Smith for the Judge to try, or not."

"Find him where?"

"Western Arkansas, Indian Territory, or Kansas…maybe Missouri. No, just Arkansas, the Territory, or Kansas."

"Just those three? Do you know how big that area is?"

"Yep. I got an idea."

"I like hotels, towns, dining rooms, and saloons. There are not a lot of those where we are going."

"Nope."

"I give up. You let me stand there and promise to be a Deputy U.S. Marshal, and go after a disreputable killer without a so much as asking if I really wanted to do that?"

"Yep."

"Here. Take this badge back to the Judge." Isaac slaps his marshal's badge on the table in front of Chad.

"Nope. Can't do that. Gotta go to the livery and pick out a horse that you can get familiar with. You're gonna be spendin' a lot of time ridin' 'em." Chad stands and walks to the dining room doorway.

"Never, never, never did I think this could happen to me…a Deputy U.S. Marshal." Isaac snatches his badge off the table, slips it into his vest pocket, stands, and follows Chad.

The newborn sun shatters the darkness as morning washes wave after wave of sparkling daylight across the grass covered plains. In the shallow valley, a man kneels striking a match to kindling piled in a fire pit. A blossom of flame erupts, and the man heaps on small pieces of wood to keep the fire growing.

"Get up, Victor. We've got miles to go today." Rafe kicks the man rolled up in his blanket beside the fire.

"Aiy, amigo. Must you get up with the sun?" Victor rolls over tightening his blanket about himself.

"Suit yourself, I'm fixin' some grub and leavin.'"

"All right, all right, I'm getting up." Victor throws off his blanket, sits up, and picks up his boot. He turns it upside down knocking out any critters that took up residence inside it overnight, slides it on his foot, and repeats it with the second boot. He stands, stomps both feet, and walks a short distance into the prairie to relieve himself.

Rafe has coffee boiling in the pot he's placed on the fire. His canteen lies beside him. The spitting, spatting, and aroma of frying bacon fills the air as he stirs slices around in the frying pan he holds over the fire.

Victor returns, rolls up his bedding, and ties both ends. He grabs a tin cup from his saddlebag, slaps it against his leg to knock out any dirt, carefully tips the coffee pot, and fills his cup. Warming both hands around the cup, he sips at the steaming coffee, and watches the sun rise.

"Hey, amigo. How far is it to Dodge City?"

"If we ride hard today, we should get there by early evening." Rafe fishes a slice of bacon out of the skillet with a fork, blows on it to cool, and carefully nibbles the crispy pork.

"It will be good to sleep in a bed again, no?"

"Yeah, kinda lookin' forward to that myself."

"You were lucky to sell those cattles to ol' Doan at Red River. It made travel much quicker, yes?"

"Weren't luck, amigo. I know'd ol' Doan would snap up them cattle. He's a bigger rustler than we are. Only he don't get caught. He does things like write up bills of sale and such to claim he's a legitimate cattleman."

"If you hadn't shot that cowboy at Doby Springs, we could have stayed there."

"Why'd you want to stay there? It ain't nothin' but a few mud wattle huts and a brokedown saloon. Besides, that cowboy needed killin'. Ain't nobody gonna brace me like that and walk away."

"*Si*, that may be, amigo, but you shoots him in the back when he walks away. Them other hombres, they want to kill us."

"Good thing you cut the cinch straps on their horses tied up out front of the saloon, or else they'd have rode us down for certain."

"*Si*, I have learned some things that help. But, amigo, I will not help you again if you burn another man."

"Don't go gettin' squeamish on me. It was only a sodbuster, and he was tryin' to farm where he don't belong."

"He lived in the dugout along the creek bank and farmed a small plot of land, amigo. He was of no bother to us or anybody."

"He was a sodbuster, and they don't deserve to live."

"So you say, amigo, but you shoots him and hangs him and then burns him. That is too much."

"Shut up, eat your breakfast. We gotta ride." Rafe throws the grease from the frying pan into the fire. A plume of flame and smoke billows upward.

The rhythmic clacking of the wheels of the Atchison, Topeka, and Santa Fe train on the track along with the rocking motion of the Pullman coach are almost hypnotic. If not for the constant noise of the other passengers, Chad knows he'd be asleep. He's amazed that Isaac seems to master tuning everything out and appears to sleep soundly, sitting upright with his chin resting on his chest. The next stop is Dodge City, Kansas. Isaac's voice slips from under his pulled down hat brim.

"Feels like we are approaching our destination. The vibrations are changing."

"I suppose it won't be long now. Thought you were asleep."

"I tried to. Did for a bit. A lot of noise keeps me from sleeping too deeply." Isaac pushes his hat back and scoots up on the seat. "Hard to keep twenty people quiet in this shoe box of a coach, and that lady with two kids, four rows back, has her hands full."

"Yep. If one ain't cryin', the other one's screamin', and the four men at the back make enough noise for ten with their never endin' poker game."

Scattered on the landscape, buildings begin coming into view. Soon the train slows approaching Dodge City. The depot is a fifteen by fifty foot, whitewashed, single storied, wooden structure with equally divided areas. A waiting area is on one end, the office for the railroad agent and telegrapher in the middle, and a storage room is located on the opposite end. A sign hangs from the eve of the roof with the name *Dodge City, Kansas,* painted on it. An extended platform surrounds the depot on all sides. It's littered and stacked high with boxes and barrels of every size and shape, multi-sized crates, and stacks of farming equipment covered with tarps. Chad stands on the steps of the railcar between coaches surveying the accumulated freight as he waits for the train to come to a complete stop.

From the front, a loud burst of steam from the engine announces their arrival. Rattling and groaning, the train comes to a jolting halt.

"Come on, Isaac. We've got to unload our horses, mule, and supplies." Chad steps onto the platform.

"Reluctantly, I'm right behind you. Riding this train, with all of its annoyances is still preferable to the conveyance we are about to utilize."

"After five or ten miles, you'll become saddle hardened again. Remember, you rode the Chisholm Trail."

"Primarily seated in a wagon if you'll recall."

"On the way to Abilene you did, but not returning."

"Yes, that is correct, and I believe that is what has so affected my disdain for being horseback."

"Oh, quit your whinin'. We've got to get loaded and find the marshal. Come on."

Quickly, Chad walks to the stock car and talks with the conductor and stockman about unloading their mounts. He returns to the platform where Isaac waits.

"All right, the stock will be unloaded and in the corral in the next hour. We can go to grab a bite and a beer while we wait for them."

"Sounds like your best idea today. Lead the way."

Chad steps to the rear of the platform as Isaac follows and looks down the main street of Dodge City.

Wooden, single and two-story, many false fronted buildings line both sides of a dirt roadway. Board sidewalks provide a means to walk without wading through the muddy quagmire during the rainy season.

Chad sees signs hanging from buildings or painted on the walls, identifying the establishments as saloons, gambling halls, general stores, morticians, barbers, or brothels.

A placard nailed up to the station wall advertises a bull-fighting ring where Mexican matadors put on displays with Longhorn bulls. He points it out to Isaac who looks and rolls his eyes.

Horseback riders travel up and down Main Street. Freight wagons lumber along, stopping periodically to load and unload merchandise on the boardwalk. Many buckboard wagons carrying ranching and farming supplies bounce along the rutted street, dodging traffic. A few covered wagons have families, along with their worldly possessions, threading their way through the clusters of people, horses, piles of lumber, and wagons along the main thoroughfare. Creaking harness noises, dirt, dust, shouting, cursing, bullwhip snapping, and horses whinnying add to the chaos and confusion.

"Seems like a right lively place, don't it?" Chad pauses as he looks for a café sign.

"I had a conversation with a rider on the train who said Dodge City is acquiring a reputation for being a gunfighter's town."

"Wouldn't be surprised. Both the Chisholm and Western Trails run herds into the loading pens. Cowboys, whiskey, and money bring on troubles."

"They said the stockyards are the largest west of St. Louis, and they are expecting a minimum of 200,000 head of cattle this season."

"That would explain all the signs advertising stock agents." Chad points out wooden shingles swinging in the breeze from arms attached to building fronts.

"The train rider also said if we are staying for any time at all, we need to rent rooms at the Dodge House hotel. He claimed it is the best accommodations this side of St. Louis."

"Sounds like that would be fine, but we need to find the marshal, Wyatt Earp. I have to find out what he knows about Rafe Dolin."

"You do that, and I'll check out the Longbranch Saloon. I understand it is the best in town."

"I'd expect a whiskey peddler to want to go there."

"I've told you over and over that I never peddled whiskey. I am a certified pharmacist and provided medicinal elixir and remedies. I give up. Okay, I've been a whiskey peddler. Are you satisfied?"

"Now, Isaac don't get your britches in a twist. I have more fun yankin' your chain than you can imagine. I know you are a bonafide pharmacist, but it don't mean I can't have fun at your expense."

"Go find your Marshal Earp. That certainly is a strange name."

"Any stranger than Wisenheimer?"

"Touche."

"Touch…what?"

"Just go, go, and I'll wait at the Longbranch, and don't take all day about it." Isaac stomps along the board sidewalk heading for the saloon.

Chad crosses the street, dodges horsemen and wagons, and looks for the jail sign. Spotting it, he walks rapidly along the boardwalk, dodging other pedestrians.

He approaches a brick building with barred windows and a solid wooden door. Grabbing the handle, he opens the door, and steps inside.

"Can I help you, stranger," a voice asks.

Chad focuses, his eyes adjusting to the dimly lit interior,

and sees a man seated behind the desk in a blue flannel shirt, hatless, balding, and smoking on a thin cigarillo. On the desk lies a Colt Peacemaker within easy reach.

"I'll only ask one more time, stranger. Can I help you?"

"If you're the sheriff, I hope so," answers Chad, closing the door behind him. "I'm lookin' for Marshal Wyatt Earp. Is he around?"

"If you mean Assistant Marshal Earp, it depends. Who are you?"

"Marshal Westerman. Judge Parker sent me to find Marshal Earp." Chad pulls his coat back to display the badge pinned to his shirt pocket.

With a hearty laugh, the man behind the desk leans back. "So old Isaac Parker is sending marshals our direction now? I thought he had his hands full with the Territory."

"Well, you might say I'm on special assignment." Chad moves toward the chair in front of the desk. "Mind if I sit, sheriff…"

"I'm Larry Deger, Marshal of Dodge City. Take the load off, but don't plan on stayin' long."

"I won't, Marshal."

"Just how special of an assignment are you on?"

"Can't rightly say. That's what I need to see Marshal Earp about."

"Uh-huh, and that don't include me. Well, well."

"Nothin' personal, Marshal. Judge Parker just told me to talk with Earp. You didn't say if he was hereabouts."

"Nope, I didn't did I?"

"Marshal, I'm not lookin' for trouble. I just need to talk with Earp and then leave your fair town."

"You'll find him at the Longbranch most likely. He deals

Faro in his spare time."

"Obliged." Chad stands and steps to open the door.

"Have your conversation, and then leave, Marshal Westerman. I've already got enough buffalo hunters, cowboys, gunslingers, pimps, card sharps, settlers, and *marshals* to deal with in Dodge City."

Chad nods, opens the door, steps outside, and closes the door behind him. He pauses looking up and down the street.

I've been in a few places, but this one ain't the friendliest by a long shot. I'll look up Earp, get Isaac, and we'll shake the dust of this place from our boots quick-like.

5

LONGBRANCH

WALKING ALONG THE BOARD SIDEWALK, CHAD IS enthralled by the constant motion of people in Dodge. The boardwalk is crowded, people enter and leave stores, the wagons and horses travel Main Street. It seems the entire town is in motion. He hears the piano playing before rounding the corner and reaching the Longbranch saloon. It's being played poorly.

The rowdy noise of men drinking, gambling, and singing spills through the batwing doorway.

Chad pauses to look into the saloon through a large plate glass window. The bar rail stretches from front to back of the space along the left side. In the back is a raised stage with crimson drapes and backdrop. A line of women dances on the stage, doing the can-can to the thrill of the male audience assembled before them. Beside the stage sits a piano with the player pounding away on the keys. Scattered around the open area are tables with chairs. On the right side, roulette, dice, and wheels of chance tables line the wall. Six Faro tables sit close to the front door. Men line the bar drinking. Some have a foot propped on a brass rail that runs the length along the base of the mahogany counter. Spittoons are strategically placed beside tables to catch tobacco juice. The floor is stained around them with more misses than hits. A pallor of cigarette and cigar smoke hangs in the air keeping the saloon in a perpetual fog.

Looks like a right lively place. Earp's in here somewhere.

Chad spots Isaac standin' beside a Faro table, shoves open the batwing doors, and walks into the saloon. "Isaac, looks like you've made yourself to home."

"Shhhh. Pay attention. This is some game to watch." Isaac points at the Faro table where men, seated and standing, place bets on the cards painted on the table top. "Watch the dealer, he knows exactly where each bet is, how much, and sweeps the board, paying winners and collecting from losers. It is a real sight to behold."

"It's probably the only game you'd have a chance at winning."

"I've been trying to figure out what is going on with little success."

"All right, here's the way it plays. There's one dealer, or banker, and any number of players. Each player places his stake on one of the thirteen cards on the board. Every player can place bets on the same or multiple cards when they slip their coins between them or sit on the edge of a card. They can also place a bet in the high card box. Are you followin' along?"

"Yes, but, watching all the hands and coins move everywhere

on the board looks to be almost impossible."

"A good dealer has got to eyeball all of them."

"I am impressed."

"All right, a full deck is shuffled and placed in the 'shoe,' a dealing box, to keep the dealer honest. Two cards are drawn out of the shoe. The first card is the dealer's and goes to the right side of the shoe. Everyone who bets that card on the dealer's board loses their money to the bank. The second card is the player's card and is placed on the left side of the shoe. Everyone who bets that card is paid dollar for dollar. If anyone is playing the high card box and the player's card is higher than the banker's, they win also."

"I must give this game of chance a gentleman's try."

"Well, if you've got to, then here's my advice. Take a good look at the money you're gonna wager and give it a kiss goodbye. If it comes back, pick it up and walk away. If it's gone, you've learned a lesson. Who's the dealer?"

"I can't say we have been introduced. He has been concentrating on the game, speaks seldom, and seems completely competent."

"When he takes a break, ask if he knows Wyatt Earp. I'm goin' to the bar for a beer." Chad moves through the jostling crowd toward the bar.

Chad finds a place at the bar after shouldering between two inebriated patrons. He places one foot on the brass rail along the bottom of the counter and orders a beer from the bartender. As he is about to take a sip, gunfire explodes on the street in front of the saloon. In reaction, Chad reaches for his revolver and turns to face the entrance.

Through the swinging door stomps a young cowboy along with three compadres, all wearing sweat stained Stetsons, flapping chaps, spur rowels ringing on the floor as they walk, and dust covered bib-front shirts. The lead cowboy has each hand filled with a revolver and shoots at the ceiling.

"Herd's in the loadin' pens, gents. We come all the way from San Antonio and are dry enough to drink this establishment plumb out of whiskey. Yeeeehawwwww." He fires his pistols repeatedly then drops them into the holsters strapped around his waist.

Chad releases the grip on his Colt and watches the cowboys saunter up to the bar, and pound on the counter.

"Barkeep," shouts the cowboy. "Give me a bottle of Old Grand Dad and three glasses. And make 'em clean ones." He turns and leans again the bar. Chad looks at the boots with large rowlded spurs, dirty chaps, Levi's, shirt, and vest the man wears. A round crown hat with wide brim covers brown hair.

"A hard drive, cowboy?" Chad asks.

"Ha. It was just long. I ate enough dust for a while. Time to drink." The cowboy grabs the bottle and glasses from the bar tender and moves toward the table his friends sit at. The room settles back into the cacophony of sound it was at before the cowboy's arrival.

Chad picks up his beer and moves to a nearby table to join Isaac and the Faro dealer.

The man has well-manicured hands, a black frock coat, a white shirt with stiff celluloid collar, and a silk cravat style necktie with stickpin that distinguish him from farmers, cowboys, and other patrons of the saloon. His blond hair is short and carefully combed. Heavy eyebrows rest above piercing blue eyes, and a full handlebar style mustache covers his upper lip.

"Chadbourne, let me introduce Wyatt Earp." Isaac motions Chad to take a seat.

"Assistant Marshal Wyatt Earp, I'm glad to meet you." Chad extends his right hand.

"Marshal Chadbourne Westerman, the pleasure is mine." Earp appears at ease and friendly as he grasps Chad's hand in a hearty handshake. His eyes continue to sweep the saloon taking in all actions and people in the place. "To what do I owe this privilege?"

"Judge Parker from Fort Smith says you are familiar with an outlaw we are trailin'. The jasper is named Rafe Dolin."

"Dolin. Oh yes, he's been in Dodge City a number of times. We've had a few minor altercations. Seems a mite too friendly, spends money like water, and I wouldn't turn my back on him."

"Would you mind describing him for me?"

"Sure. Nothing unusual to tell. He dresses like a cowboy in Levis, worn-out boots, and a dirty gray cavalry hat with tassels. Seems to be particularly attached to a filthy black duster. Never did hear why. He looks like any other saddle tramp riding through, looking to make a name for himself. We've got way too many gun sharps in Dodge; don't need any more. Why the interest?"

"He's a killer, a murderer, rustler, rapist, and man-burner. Judge Parker wants him in Fort Smith for trial."

"Not surprised. If I see him in town again, I'll lock him up and get word to you."

"So, he's not here now?"

"Nope. He was here, might have been a couple months ago. Some of the breed that hang with him said he was headed for Texas."

"He's been there and gone. I figure he's in the Territory wandering back and forth from here to there."

"Likely. Can I do any more for you?"

"Not right now, Marshal. Isaac and I will be headin' for Indian Territory in the morning."

"Can't say I envy you. The Territory is no place to linger."

"Thank you, Marshal. Look us up in Texas whenever you're down that direction."

"Much obliged, gentlemen. Enjoy Dodge City, and then leave like my boss Marshal Deger always tells new arrivals." Earp laughs out loud.

"I had the pleasure of meeting your Marshal Deger today. Can't say it was a real treat. We'll spend tonight at Dodge House and head out in the morning."

"Have a safe trip and good hunting." Earp rises and moves to an open Faro table and begins setting up for his next game.

Chad and Isaac stand and leave the saloon heading toward the Dodge House.

The Territory stretches before the two riders. Rolling grass covered hills, shallow valleys with walnut, oak, and cottonwood groves, thickets of mayhaw and hackberry, and solitary homesteads and small ranches scatter on the landscape.

"Why didn't we go to Dodge City," asks Victor as he lopes along beside Rafe.

"Don't know. Just didn't feel right."

"Where are we headin' now?"

"East."

"I know the direction, where are we goin'?"

"Got a job to take care of that direction."

"There's a whole lot of nuthin' between here and there."

"Yep, I reckon you're right."

"Are you runnin' from somebody?"

"Been runnin' for a long time. Anybody who tries to stop me dies, sometimes quick, sometimes slow."

"You worried about *indios* our here?"

"Nope. I'll just kill 'em."

"What about a whole passel of them?"

"Kill 'em all, right down to the last one."

"Somethin' just ain't right with you."

"Yep. Since I lost my pards at the Arkansas River, everybody dies."

"Ain't I your pard?"

"Shut up and ride."

Rafe spurs his horse into a gallop up a steep slope.

Victor pulls his horse up, twists around, and checks their back trail. Nobody follows them. Turning around, he spurs his horse to catch up with Rafe.

6

TERRITORY

ISAAC WALKS DOWN THE STAIRCASE THAT LEADS FROM THE second floor sleeping rooms in the Dodge House. His saddlebags hang over his shoulder. Below him, the lobby is already a beehive of early morning activities with cattle buyers' agents meeting trail bosses and arranging purchases of herds, travelers attempting to check out and make the morning train departure, and businessmen conducting transactions with drummers selling goods. A scurry of people rush through the lobby into the dining room, taking their business to the breakfast table.

Isaac looks for Chad.

He spots him tucked into an overstuffed chair in the corner reading a newspaper. Chad thumbs through the pages as Isaac approaches.

"'Bout time you wandered this direction." Chad turns another page.

"It was difficult to leave that brass bed this morning. The down coverlet and feather pillows made sleeping much more preferable than riding a horse."

"Yeah, yeah, and the washstand with basin and pitcher and comfortable side chair held you in the room, right?"

"They did have their own attraction."

"Did you try out the bathtub at the end of the hallway?" Chad folds his paper and lays it in his lap.

"It was amazing. Hot water actually gushed out of the faucet when I turned one handle and cold came out when I turned the other."

"I could dunk you in a creek a whole lot easier."

"New inventions mean progress."

"If you say so."

"There's a lot that does not seem right to me as well, but I am too hungry to discuss them right now. Let's get some breakfast." Isaac walks past Chad into the dining room. Chad stands, sticks his paper under his arm, and follows.

I don't care what you think Isaac, maybe progress ain't all it's cracked up to be.

The hot sun beats down on two riders crossing the grass covered hills, heading toward the cattle trail borough of Doby Springs.

"Chad, it's been two days riding south on this cattle trail.

Why are we doing this?"

"It stands to reason that if Dolin rustled cattle in Texas, he's either heading them to the railroad in Kansas or looking for a buyer. If we follow the trail south, we might just run smack into him. If we don't, maybe we can pick up on his trail."

"There are times when I wish you were not so logical. It makes arguing with you very difficult."

"I'm just thinkin' about what I would do in the same situation. If that's logical, then now I know what to call it."

"We have not heard anything about Dolin in the last couple of hovels we passed through. What makes you think this one up ahead will be different?"

"We're 'bout there so it can't hurt to stop and ask."

Chad and Isaac ride into the wattle huts of Doby Springs and step off their mounts, tie them to the hitching rail, and walk through the open doorway into the ramshackle saloon.

A six-foot pine board rests on barrels at either end, two decrepit tables barely stand, and a pair of broken chairs sit at each table. A slack-jawed, bearded man stands behind the bar. He wears a filthy apron tied around his waist and an equally dirty cotton pullover shirt. The rag he mops around the bar top is dirtier than his apron.

"Ain't got much, gents. Red eye, that's it."

"Not really interested, friend," replies Chad. "We're looking for someone. He may have passed your direction."

"Don't give information. Don't have to. It ain't healthy."

"You're right. I don't blame you."

"Damned right."

"What if I ask about a fellar in a black duster, wearin' a cavalry hat with tassels, travelin' with a Mexican partner. Is there any chance of somebody like that driftin' through here lately?"

"You're a sly one, ain't you?"

"Ain't any slyer than the next cowboy, friend."

"What if somebody like that did drift through?" The bar owner smears dirt on the counter around.

"Then if someone knew where he went, it might be worth say, five dollars."

"What if that someone killed some cowboys while he was here?"

"That's a hangin' offense, friend. I'm duty bound to see him taken before Judge Parker in Fort Smith for trial."

"'Hangin' Judge Parker'?"

"Yep."

"Well, I'll be. Make it ten dollars."

"That man was here?"

"Yep. Killed two cowboys that braced him about bein' from Texas. Shot both of 'em in the back. That Mex he rides with sliced the cinch straps on the horses out front. They got away scot free."

"Any idea where he headed?"

"Some boys came in a while ago sayin' they saw two riders heading east, the duster and a sombrero wearer. The ten dollars?"

"Pay the man, Isaac. Much obliged, friend." Chad turns and leaves the saloon.

Isaac slaps a gold eagle on the pine board bar top and hustles after Chad.

The rolling hills, forested valleys, and grassy prairie stretches as far as can be seen. It's been a full day since leaving Doby Springs, and Chad keeps pushing his horse, resting briefly to keep from running his mount into the ground.

"Chadbourne, we've got to stop, refresh ourselves, and rest our horses. It does no good risking everything and then being afoot out here in this endless expanse. Are you listening to me?" Isaac shifts in his saddle trying to find a comfortable position.

"I hear you, and you're right; I just hate bein' close to Dolin and let him slip away. You see that clump of oaks in the valley ahead of us? We'll pull up there."

"Finally, common sense prevails. I think I've become molded to the back of this horse."

"High time your takin' to riding, Isaac. High time."

Chad rides into the trees in the shallow valley, dismounts, undoes his horse's cinch, and drops the saddle to the ground. He hobbles his horse and turns it out to graze. Isaac does the same with his horse and the pack mule.

Coffee aroma fills the air beside the small campfire. Isaac is stretched out on the ground with his head resting on his bedroll. Chad sits with his back propped against the nearby walnut tree. Their horses graze quietly close by.

"We are between the Canadian and North Branch of the Canadian Rivers. Just a ways east of us is Seminole Town. I'm guessin' that Dolin and the Mex are followin' along the

Canadian headin' east."

"What makes you think that?"

"It's what I'd be doing. Ridin' between these rivers keeps bein' surprised by others to a minimum and provides water and grazin' for your horses."

"So, you are proposing we keep heading east all the way to Fort Smith?"

"You know, it don't take a whole wall to fall on you does it?"

"Sometimes, half of a wall will do." Isaac sighs and pulls his hat over his eyes.

Chad smirks.

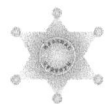

The men lie on the hilltop, watching the farmer work his plow around the end of the field and cluck his team into lining up a new furrow. About two dozen rows, each thirty feet long, have been dug into the rich prairie sod.

"Seminole Town is only over the next hill, Rafe. It is time to go, *amigo*." Victor starts to stand and is pulled back down by Rafe.

"That there is a sodbuster. He ain't got no business diggin' up Indian Territory like this."

"Maybe the Seminoles sold him the land, or he could be Indian, or who cares?"

"I care, and I aim to do somethin' about it."

"*Amigo*, I told you I'm not seein' you burn another farmer. *Mi familia esta* farmers."

"You're not all that clean, my Mex friend. I know that they

got paper out on you for killin' cowboys down in the Creek Indian territory. You cover my back as much as I cover yours."

"*Si, si,* I'm sure the marshals they look for both of us."

"You stay here. I'll be back." Rafe pushes back from the edge of the hilltop, stands, and mounts his horse. He looks back at Victor. "Stay put or I won't take it kindly."

"*Si, amigo.* Go do what you must. I'll wait over in the grove of trees."

"You do that. I'll be back." Rafe turns his horse and slowly begins walking down the hill toward the farmer.

The hot sun beats mercilessly down on the man behind the plow as he wrestles to keep it upright and cutting in a straight line. He grabs the reins around his shoulder and tugs on it stopping the horse. Raising his hand to shield his eyes, he watches the stranger approach.

"Howdy." He wraps the reins around the plow handle and steps from behind the plow to get a better look at the approaching rider. "You from around here?"

Rafe continues to walk his horse and stops in front of the farmer. He leans forward and rests his arms on his saddle horn.

"You're cuttin' up the open range, friend."

"I purchased fifty acres from the Seminoles. My wife is a member of the tribe. We're fixin to make our home and farm this land. It's right fine land. I got some cool creek water in the jug by that brush pile of timber if you want a drink."

"You cut out all those trees by yourself?" Rafe looks at the tree stumps and tall pile of timber stacked about twenty yards behind the farmer.

"Yep. I been at it a while. Got a can of coal oil over there to burn out the stumps."

"I've never seen that done before. Does it work good?"

"Not the best, but it beats trying to dig 'em out."

"Your wife help?"

"As best she can, but she's back at the dugout beside the creek over the hill."

"Well, maybe I'll just go visit her once we're finished here."

"What do you mean?" The farmer watches Rafe's hand edge toward his pistol. He looks around for a weapon and realizes his rifle is too far away, lying beside the jug of water. His panic-stricken eyes dart around seeking cover or help. "Look mister, I ain't hurtin' nobody or nothin'. Just leave me be."

"Looks like it just ain't your day, friend." Rafe yanks his pistol out and shoots the farmer in the right leg.

Crying out in pain, the man grabs his leg as he falls to the ground. "Why'd you do that? Leave me alone. Don't shoot again," he shrieks as he attempts to scoot behind his plow.

Rafe levels his pistol and shoots the man in his other leg. Then he fires again, hitting the farmer's right arm, and then his left.

The man lies on the ground screaming, crying and cursing. He attempts to move but can't rise from the furrows. Blood pools around him. He shouts at Rafe. "Why? Why? I never did anything to you. I'll kill you. I'll kill you."

"I don't reckon I've got to worry about you plowin' any more open range now, do I?" A hysterical howl escapes Rafe. Kicking his horse into a walk, he rides to the timber and brush pile, reaches down from his saddle, and lifts the can of coal oil. He rides back to the incapacitated man and liberally douses him.

The farmer watches in horror and feebly tries to wipe the coal oil from his face with his shoulder.

Pulling out a Lucifer, Rafe strikes it on his pistol handle and looks at the squirming man on the ground.

"No. No. Don't do it. I beg you. I beg you. Don't do it." The farmer screams in horror.

Rafe tosses the match onto the man's saturated bib overalls. An instantaneous whoosh of kerosene ignites, drowning out his screams. He continues to shriek and crawl frantically away as flames leap skyward.

Then, silence.

The farmer lies still.

The fire snaps and crackles.

Rafe turns his horse away from the man, pulls his pistol, and shoots the plow horse in the head. The animal drops into a heap.

Ain't no need for this horse to plow. Now, that job's done. Time to find the wife. Rafe spurs his horse and rides up the hill.

7

GETTING ACQUAINTED

ISAAC POINTS TO THE CIRCLING BIRDS IN THE CLOUDLESS blue sky.

"Buzzards," says Chad.

"Does not bode good, does it?" Isaac watches the birds glide silently through the sky.

"They ain't there without a reason. Let's find out." Chad spurs his horse into a lope, riding over the hill. Isaac trails behind him.

Cresting the hill, they see a plot of turned ground, a plow, a dead horse, brush pile, and a burnt spot with something charred in the middle of it. Beside the burned spot stands a man holding the reins of his large white horse.

They descend the hillside and slowly walk their horses toward the negro standing beside the charred remains.

"Howdy," says Chad raising a hand in welcome.

The stranger looks up from under his large brimmed hat and acknowledges the greeting. "Howdy."

Chad sees the rider is at least six feet tall. He wears gray trousers, a blue flannel shirt, a black vest, a holstered pistol, black boots, and has a handlebar moustache.

"Looks like you've had trouble, friend." Chad figures he's a cowboy from a nearby cattle drive or ranch.

"Not my troubles," the man replies. "More like that poor soul's, but he don't worry about nothin' no more." He points at the charred remains.

"My God, that is a person, or it was a person." Isaac stares in wonder at the burned body.

Chad eases his hand toward his revolver. "You know who that is?"

"Don't be too quick on the trigger. I just rode up like y'all." The man steps sideways ready to draw his pistol.

"Who are you?" Chad stops his horse.

"Who wants to know?" The man doesn't flinch.

"I'm U.S. Marshal Chadbourne Westerman, friend. Who are you?"

"Well, I'll be. Marshal Westerman, I'm U.S. Marshal Bass Reeves."

"This here is Marshal Isaac Wisenheimer." Chad motions toward his partner.

"Climb on down and take a look with me. It appears the man was set on fire. The coal oil can is over there." Bass points to the can lying up the hill. "Don't know why somebody would be plowin' and set himself on fire. The brush pile is over yonder. Don't make sense."

Chad steps off his horse and walks to the body. He examines

the corpse closely. "This fella appears to have been plowin' and then burnt. Who shot the horse?"

"Who would do such a detestable thing?" Isaac watches from his saddle.

Bass Reeves looks at Chad. "Only one man-burner I know in the Territory right now. That's Rafe Dolin and his partner Victor Gonzales."

"You trailin' them?" asks Chad.

"I got papers on Gonzales, but I'll take Dolin down as well."

"Dolin has an appointment with the rope in Judge Parker's court in Fort Smith," says Chad.

"I'm ten days out of Fort Smith. Sent two other outlaws in on the jail wagon the other day. I'm stayin' out to catch Gonzales."

"I want Dolin."

"He's a bad one, Marshal. I come up on a homestead just over the hill. It's a dugout, and all torn up. The woman, a Seminole, was stripped, strapped over a barrel, and looked like they had their way with her, beaten bad, knife slices all over her body, her breasts cut off, and her throat sliced. Hopefully, during the start of her torture she died. I wrapped her up in a blanket and buried her. Gonzales is a knife-man."

"What is this place? Who would do such things to these people?" Isaac is dumbfounded.

"He's new out here?" Bass gestures toward Isaac.

"Yep, new to marshalin', but comin' along fine."

"He better toughen up. This here is what the Territory is all about. The worst of the worst are here, and they ain't gettin' any better by the day."

"It'll be an education for him, that's for sure. Bass, I'll bury this man. Let's find cover for the night in the grove down the valley and decide what to do next."

"That'll be fine by me, Marshal. It's been a long day."

The campfire pops and snaps as Chad adds limbs to the blaze. Bedrolls are unrolled beside the firepit, horses are hobbled and graze close by. Fatback sizzles in a fry pan.

Bass pats out johnny cakes. He places each in a greased skillet. "My wife taught me to make Shawnee cakes years ago. I've just takin' a hankering to them."

"It all smells delicious," says Isaac inhaling deeply.

Chad stretches out on his bedroll. "What brings you this direction, Bass."

"Like I told you earlier, Gonzales. I've crossed his path too many times, always ugly. Got Judge Parker to issue a warrant, been carryin' it in my pack."

"Looks like we're not far behind Dolin and Gonzales. Where do you think they might be headin'?"

"Eufaula, probably."

"Ain't that an old Creek Indian town?"

"Sure is."

"Why do you think they're headin' there?"

"What I've found out is that Gonzales tends to stay out for a while, then wander back to town. He's a townbody. Prefers finer things like a good bed, a roof over his head, food, and his choice of whores. He'll be headin' for Eufaula."

"Besides, the Missouri-Kansas-Texas railroad reaches there? That's another reason for them to head to Eufaula. They can catch a train from there." He picks up a cake from a tin plate sitting on a firepit stone and tosses it to Chad. "Hot stuff, catch."

"Don't leave me out, Marshal Reeves," Isaac holds out his hand.

Bass looks at Chad. "You sure you want to ride with him?"

"Got too much time invested in him already. Got to see it through." Chad smiles.

"Gentlemen, I'm sitting right here. I'm not invisible." Isaac takes a bite of his cake.

"How'd you get into marshalin' for Judge Parker, Bass?" Chad rolls over onto his side.

"During the war, I escaped from Texas and lived with the Creek and Seminole Indians in the Territory. After the Emancipation, I moved to Arkansas, raised a family—ten kids. Right happy with life. Then Parker came lookin' for marshals to clean up the territory. That was in '75. Been ridin' for Judge Parker ever since. What about you?"

"Was a drover as a kid. Took herds up the Chisholm Trail. Took a job as range detective and that led to U.S. Marshalin'. An acquaintance gave my name to Judge Parker. He called me to Fort Smith, and now I'm trailin' Dolin to put him out of business. Fixin' to get back to Texas as soon as I can."

"What about your partner?"

"Need I remind you gentlemen that I'm sitting right here?"

"Well then, speak up, Isaac." Chad rolls onto his back and pulls his hat over his eyes.

"I am a certified pharmacist by profession. My semi-civilized partner accosted me outside of Fredericksburg a few years ago and impressed me into his service. We traveled to Dodge City, then back to Texas. He became a U.S. Marshal, and I followed him to Fort Smith. He diabolically arranged for Judge Parker to swear me in as a marshal. I'm still not clear on how all that happened. Here I am."

"You're one of a few now, my reluctant friend." Chad speaks from under his hat.

"He's right, pharmacist. There's a little less than two hundred of us covering over seventy-five thousand miles of Indian Territory. It ain't an easy job, but it's got to be done."

"After what I've seen, I understand the necessity but am definitely uncomfortable with the risk."

"Ah hell, pharmacist, you can't live forever." Bass laughs out loud and lays down on his bedroll, pulling his hat over his eyes.

Isaac rolls up in his blanket and settles his head on his saddle for a pillow. He considers Reeves' last comment. *Well, I intend to make certain it is absolutely as long as humanly possible, and then even a little longer.*

8

TRAILING

C HAD AND BASS ARE UP BEFORE DAYBREAK. THEY
load their gear on the pack mule, drag Isaac from
his blankets, and greet the first rays of sunshine that
splash across the horizon.

The rising morning sun lights up the hilly landscape as the
three riders lope their horses toward Eufaula. They hear the
gunfire.

The rifle blasts again, and the bullet sends bark flying from the
tree where Rafe is hiding. Beside him, behind another tree,

Victor keeps his eye on a wagon stacked high with crates and open boxes. A mule in front of the wagon lies dead, still in his harness. Beside the mule stands another, nervously flicking its ears and tail as bullets fly through the air.

"Calm down old timer, we just come lookin' for some whiskey," shouts Rafe.

"You came to steal my wagon you miserable bushwhackers." The wagon driver hides in the boot under the seat of the wagon. His rifle is in his hands. He is older with a weathered face. He wears a dirty buckskin jacket over a dingy white long john shirt. His filthy levis are ripped and torn in many places. Clear blue eyes sight along the rifle barrel as he squeezes off another shot. "You come out from behind those trees and you're both dead men."

"What now, *amigo*," says Victor hugging his tree for cover.

"That damned whiskey peddler would have let us ride up except for you bein' a Mex."

"Hey, *amigo*, you are the one that pulls his *pistola*."

"That was because he was figuring to ventilate you. Now, shut up and shoot."

Both men step from behind their trees and fire rapidly at the man in the wagon, then they step back for cover. A moan comes from the wagon.

"Hey, peddler, you don't sound so good," shouts Rafe. "I think one of us plugged you."

"Step out...ahhh...again you damned...ahhh...thief. I'll kill you for sure." The moan grows louder.

"Don't think you're gonna be shootin' nobody, old man." Rafe eases from behind his tree and looks at the bullet riddled wagon. A lantern on the side is flickering flames after being struck by gunfire. Suddenly, the kerosene ignites, and the back end of the wagon explodes. The blast knocks Rafe to the ground.

"*Madre de dios,*" mutters Victor. "What happens?" He steps from behind his tree to look.

Flames whip and snap as the whiskey on the wagon begins to catch fire.

The old man pulls himself over the front edge and drops to the ground with a loud groan. Rafe walks over, grabs his jacket collar, and pulls him to the front wheel. He sits the man upright beside the wheel and, taking some rope from under the seat, he lashes both of his hands to the top of the wheel. More whiskey catches fire in the wagon and bright blue flames leap skyward.

"Didn't want to share your whiskey, did you?" Rafe sneers at the peddler. A bright red patch continues to spread across the man's midsection.

The driver grimaces and frowns. "You ain't got any, do you?"

"I'll fix that right now." Rafe reaches into a box and yanks out two bottles of whiskey. He tosses one to Victor and pulls the cork free with his teeth. He spits it out. Tipping the bottle up, he chugs three long gulps.

Rafe's eyes tear, he lowers the bottle, coughs, and speaks in a raspy voice. "This ain't fit whiskey to drink you old coyote. Hell, I wouldn't give it to an Indian."

"I wasn't fixin' to give it to nobody. I was fixin' to sell it to injuns, you damn horse's ass."

"Lettin' it burn is the right thing to do." Rafe walks back toward the trees, leaving the peddler tied to the burning wagon almost totally engulfed in flames.

"Cut me loose," screams the terror-stricken man. He tugs at the bindings holding his hands and gasps again from the gunshot wound in his stomach. "Cut me loose, you sonofabitch."

"Now, now, old man, such a temper." Rafe turns and sits on his heels watching the flames sweep down toward the man. "Times just keep getting harder for you, don't they?"

"I'll kill you, you snake. I'll kill you with my bare hands." The man draws a quaking breath, shudders, and his head drops to his chest. The flames wash down the length of the wagon as it collapses into a heap of burning coals. The peddler's body topples into the fire.

"That'll teach the old bastard to mess with me." Rafe walks toward Victor.

"The whiskey, she is not so bad. I've had worse." Victor takes another long drag from the bottle. Suddenly, the bottle explodes in his hand. Shattered glass flies in every direction. The report of a rifle echoes.

"What the hell…where did that come from?" Rafe hugs a tree for cover.

A barrage of gunfire snips limbs, twigs, and tree bark all around him.

"Get the horses, Victor. We gotta git. If we get separated, meet me in Fort Smith."

"*Si, amigo*, Fort Smith," shouts Victor. "*Adios.*"

Rafe spins around to see Victor mounted, galloping away, spurring, and whipping his horse to go faster.

"You gutless, Mex. I'll shoot you myself." He levels his pistol for a shot when bullets again strike all around him. He dives for cover.

Rafe creeps to where his horse nervously stands, stomping and whinnying. He grabs the reins, pulls the horse to him, gets a foot in a stirrup, holds the saddle horn, and using the horse as a shield, quickly moves away from the opening. When on the road to Eufaula, he swings up into the saddle and spurs the horse into a ground gulping gallop.

Chad, Bass, and Isaac stopped their horses about a hundred yards from where they heard gunfire. Creeping through the woods, they ease up to see flames flicker at the end of a wagon stacked with boxes and crates. Suddenly the contents on the end explode. Blue flames lick and flicker around the remaining items on the wagon.

"Whiskey peddler," says Bass. "That explosion just saved a lot of grief."

A man wearing a black duster ties a wounded man to the front wheel of the wagon.

"That's Dolin. Got to be him," mutters Chad.

"Over there beside the tree, wearin' the sombrero, that's Gonzales." Bass points toward the man.

"Let's go arrest them." Isaac starts to step forward. Chad reaches out and pulls him back behind a tree.

"Whoa, partner. We'll go in there just as soon as we take a look see at what's happenin'. No need to go off half-cocked and get ourselves shot."

"That is all well and good, but that wounded man is going to need assistance."

"From the looks of his shirt, he may be past helpin', and it ain't goin' to do any good to get plugged for the effort."

"Are you just going to hide here?"

"Yep and nope. Bass, you draw a bead on Gonzales. Isaac, stop talkin' and take your rifle and get ready to shoot at the black duster. We'll fire, reload, and fire another round. Ready. Do it."

Stepping into the open, the three marshals shoot at Rafe and Victor. Reload, and fire again.

"That Mexican is running. He's mounted and getting away." Bass is already on the run for his horse. "I'm on him. Y'all take care of Dolin." He steps into his saddle, yanks his horse's head up, and spurs into a gallop racing after Gonzales.

Chad and Isaac are a few steps behind. They mount and ride quickly toward the flaming wagon. Stepping down, they pull the partially scorched body of the whiskey peddler from the smoldering fire.

"Chalk up another one for Dolin." Chad walks to the mule and pulls a short shovel from the pack. "One more hole to dig. That mother's son is leavin' a trail of graves."

"It looked like he took off toward Eufaula." Isaac points toward the road leading to town.

"Yep. Gonzales lit out goin' north, and Dolin is runnin' east. Let's get this poor old soul in the ground. We got to ride hard to catch Dolin."

"Do you think Bass will catch Gonzales?"

"Ain't nobody better to do that. If he puts up a fight, Bass will make it a short one. Better still if he captures the Mex and gets him to Fort Smith for a hangin'."

"We cannot let Dolin do this again. Hurry up and dig."

"I don't see you steppin' over here to help." Chad heaves another shovelful of dirt onto a quickly growing pile.

"Somebody has to keep watch."

"Good to know that job is in good hands." Chad smiles and digs deeper.

Loping along the road leading to Eufaula, Chad and Isaac pass mile after mile of fenced farms and ranches. The closer to town, the more intense the land is being farmed.

"Looks like the railroad is bringin' in more farmers every day." Chad points at a man walking behind a double team plow.

"It certainly looks like enough of them to cultivate considerable crops."

"Yep, and farmers bring fences. No more trail drives through here."

"Do you imagine the railroad going to Dodge City will take farmers there?"

"Yep. Railroads bring farmers. Cattle drives will be a thing of the past." Chad shoves his hat back on his head.

"How long will they continue do you think?"

"Hard tellin'. The ol' Shawnee Trail from East Texas up along the west border of Arkansas into Missouri had cattle trailin' on it before the war, but farmers in Missouri blamed the Longhorns for spreadin' ticks to their livestock. The ticks carried a fever that killed their cattle, especially dairy cows."

"Is that why the herds use the Chisholm Trail?" Isaac rocks easy in the saddle keeping in synch with the horse's movement.

"Yep. Ticks, fences, and laws passed in Missouri caused the drives to move farther west. The railroad encouraged the drives by building loading pens at the railheads."

"Farmers moving west will keep the drives moving farther westward?"

"Depends. More railroads might mean we don't need drives

any more. If the cattlemen get railroads closer, why drive the cattle?" Chad resettles his hat on his head and tugs it down snug.

"Progress always changes things, doesn't it?"

"Yep. Look, town's just ahead."

Two dozen single story wood buildings line a dirt road. Another twenty or so houses surround the downtown area. Beside the main road run railroad tracks. Signboards showing saloons, general store, undertaker, bakery, café, lawyer, and other businesses swing in the wind suspended from the storefronts. Buckboards and horsemen jockey for space on the roadway. A railroad depot sits beside the train track on the edge of town. Chad heads that way.

"There's a horse that's been ridden hard." Chad looks at the lathered horse tied to the hitching rail in front of the depot. He steps from his saddle and ties his horse beside the sweat-stained animal. Isaac stops beside him.

"Do you think that is Dolin's mount?"

"Can't say. Let's check with the ticket agent." Chad walks the steps onto the platform and into the depot with Isaac right behind him.

"Can I help you men?" The agent looks up through the ticket window at Chad.

"You might be able to if you know whose mount that is outside." Chad points through the door and toward the lathered horse.

"Strangest damn thing," says the agent. "The fellow tied his horse, yanked his saddlebags, bedroll, and rifle off, and ran in here to buy a ticket. The train was ready to leave, and he jumped on. Didn't even ask where it was heading. Nothing. I don't imagine he's coming back for the horse. What do you think I should do with it?"

"I think it needs attention. Gettin' it to the livery is probably the best. Where was the train headin'?"

"To Hot Springs with a short stop in Fort Smith. Don't that beat all about that fellow?"

"I imagine he was hard pressed," says Chad. "When does the next train to Hot Springs roll through?"

"There will be another one tomorrow at ten in the morning."

"Give me two tickets for that train. Will it have a stock car? I want to take our horses."

"Oh yes, all our scheduled trains have stock cars. Here are your tickets. I would advise you to get here about one-half hour before its scheduled to leave. The morning trains are generally the most occupied."

Chad takes the tickets and pays for them.

"Thanks for the tip. Also, where's the best place to get a bed and dinner in town?"

"Personally, the best bug-free beds are at Mary's boarding house. It's a block off of Main behind the general store. Dinah's Café, beside the newspaper office, will serve you a rib-sticking meal."

"Thanks, friend. We'll see you in the morning."

Chad and Isaac leave the depot, mount up, and ride along main street searching for bed and board.

9

FORT SMITH

THE MORNING TRAIN ARRIVES ON TIME IN EUFAULA. Chad and Isaac wait at the depot, confirm their horses are loaded aboard the stock car, and board the passenger coach. The Pullman has ten rows of facing seats. Most of the seats are already taken. Chad finds two across from each other in the back end of the coach beside the potbelly stove sitting in its sandbox. Across the aisle from the heater is a closet. Chad knows inside is a one-holer with a lid. When you lift the lid, you see the railroad roadbed. He tosses his saddlebags and rifle into the storage rack above the seats. Isaac follows his actions and they take their seats as the train jolts to a start. A gray billow puffs from the engine smoke stack, and the cars jerk forward, picking up speed as the engine builds momentum.

"How do you plan on finding Dolin? What if he gets off in Fort Smith?"

"If you were an outlaw, with papers out on you, do you think you'd get off the train and wander around the town where marshals and a judge are lookin' for you?"

"You do make a very strong point."

"Dolin'll lie low. Fort Smith is just a water stop, and he'll get off at the end of the run, Hot Springs. And, before you ask, that's what I'd do."

"Okay. He gets off in Hot Springs. How do we find him?"

"Same way we always find things. Look into every place he can crawl, and then look again."

"It certainly seems that we will consume a tremendous amount of effort seeking this detestable miscreant."

"There you go again, Isaac. I'm not sure if you just make up words as you go along."

"I assure you of the veracity of my vocabulary. The words are in the English language. Unfortunately, plebian folks seem to avoid speaking properly."

"Plebian, what?"

"Lower social order."

"Oh, like me?"

"Well, I in no way intended to impugn your dignity by addressing you as plebian."

"Whether you intended to impug or insput or insult me, you sure made a good stab at it. Although, I do suppose I mangle the language somewhat."

"You definitely are not the worst by far. You just drift a bit."

"So, now you're callin' me a drifter?"

"By no means. Let us leave this subject. I would like to know what you think regarding Dolin's feeling any remorse or seeking repentance for his actions."

"You're friskier than a frog on a hot griddle jumpin' from one subject to another. Remorse? Repentance? Nope. I don't think he gives a second thought about those he kills, maims, or rapes. He's a bona fide, stone cold killer through and through."

"How do you intend to bring him to Judge Parker?"

"Don't know that I intend to."

"Are you saying you plan on killing him without a trial?"

"What I'm sayin' is that I'll get the job done. Alive or dead. Dead makes it easier."

"Does that make you any different than Dolin?"

"You are a questioning sort ain't you? Dealin' with outlaws in the Territory tends to blur the line between lawman and law breaker. Some of the best law dogs I know have walked on the other side of the line for a spell. The difference is who wears the badge."

"The badge exonerates the wearer? Is that why I am wearing a badge?"

"Let's just say that wearin' the badge is a whole lot better than runnin' from a badge wearer. You met Bass Reeves."

"Certainly, I met Marshal Reeves."

"Would you consider him a lawman?"

"In the short time we were together, I got the impression from his words and demeanor that he takes enforcing the law very personal and does it well."

"What do you mean by well?"

"He mentioned that he attempts to talk the law breaker into surrender before taking more drastic actions. Of course, there are times where choices are certainly limited."

"So, by your own admission, actions taken by lawmen are situational. Every encounter may require different tactics and plans. Sometimes the best plans end up with the outlaw or the law dog dead, or both."

"Yes, that is correct. Ah, you have made your point with Socratic logic."

"What? What's Socratic?"

"Socrates, a Greek philosopher, stated principles of logical thought by defining arguments into premise one, supporting premise two, and thereby drawing a conclusion. In your own inimitable manner, Marshal Westerman, you have done the same."

"Well, glory be. Just call me ol' Sock-rat-ees, but, do you get my drift?"

"I do, Chad. You stated it succinctly when you said, 'It is better to be the badge wearer rather than run from the badge.'"

"Good. End of philosophisin', I'm catchin' some shut-eye." Chad slumps in the seat pulling his hat over his eyes. "Wake me up before we get to Fort Smith."

As the train begins to pull out of Eufaula, a man loafing on a stack of freight crates beside the depot, rushes to the edge of the platform and judges the distance he needs to jump to reach the landing between the passenger coaches. He wears a large, round crown, floppy brimmed, sweat stained hat, and a well-worn, dirty, brown serape. The rowels of his spurs ring as he drags them over the wooden platform. A holstered pistol hangs from his side. Beside the pistol dangles a sheathed Bowie knife. His handlebar moustache droops. For a minute, he studies the distance, then leaps. He lands with a thud on the open space between the passenger coaches and quickly grabs the railing for support. Stepping across the landing and over the coach coupling, he enters the rail car.

Isaac watches the other passengers in the coach. Across from him, a young couple cuddles together, whispering to each other. He smiles remembering Abigail. Behind him two stern-faced women clutch baskets on their laps and stare out the window. The next few rows are filled with cowboys, drummers, and farmers. Four rows back, a man wearing a floppy brimmed, round crowned hat stares back at Isaac.

I can almost sense the hatred coming from that man's eyes. Who is he? Where have I seen him before? Why such animosity

A long-drawn-out wail from the locomotive whistle signals their approach to Fort Smith. He taps his boot against Chad's.

"I'm awake." The words spill out from under Chad's hat. "Heard the horn."

"Should we check with the station agent about Dolin?"

"That would be in order. Once the train stops, I'll talk with him. Should only be a twenty or thirty-minute stop giving them time to load water in the tender."

"There is a gentleman sitting a few rows back that seems intent on staring a hole through me. I do not recognize him, but he seems intent on gazing at me. Do you know who he is?"

Chad straightens up on the seat and casts a look over his left shoulder.

"Black floppy hat?"

"Yes."

"Can't say I do."

"What should I do? Go up and introduce myself to him?"

"Isaac, you never cease to amaze me. No. Don't do that. Keep an eye on him and see if he steps off the train with us."

"If he does, then what?"

"One thing at a time, Isaac. One thing at a time." Chad slouches on the seat again and pulls his hat over his eyes. "Got a few more minutes before we arrive. Let everyone get off the train before us. Keep an eye on our friend. If he moves up the aisle toward us before we stop, pull your Colt and shoot him."

"Shoot him, are you certain?"

"I'd rather him be shot than us. Wouldn't you?"

"Well, yes, but that sounds rather extreme. Maybe he is heading for the closet."

"He ain't. Just shoot him. Okay?"

"I will attempt to do as you request, reluctantly."

"Let me sleep a little bit longer." Chad feels the train's speed slowing as the locomotive rolls into the station.

Passengers depart the coach. People stand and retrieve their belongings from the overhead rack. Chad and Isaac watch the jostling and chaos of everyone's departure. During the movement, they lose sight of the man wearing the floppy hat.

"I do not see the man, Chad. People are blocking my view. He's not in his seat."

"He slid out the door on the other end of the coach. Might be waiting for us on the platform to bushwhack us, or he's simply left the train. Let's ease out and find the station agent."

Standing, Chad and Isaac step through the coach doorway, and onto the station platform. People mill around, picking up parcels and bags, greet other people, and rapidly make their way to the depot. Chad points toward the agent beside the entrance to the depot lobby. He's wearing a black suit, a white shirt, and a gold chain drapes across his vest pockets. He shakes hands with passengers who stop for a brief chat. Chad walks up.

"You're the agent?"

"Yes, sir. How can I help you?"

"Lookin' for a man." Chad pulls his jacket back to display his marshal's badge.

"Certainly, Marshal. Who are you seeking?"

"Yesterday's train from Eufaula stopped on schedule, correct?"

"Absolutely, we run a tight train schedule on the KATY line."

"Good. Did you happen to see a man wearing a black duster and a cavalry slouch hat with gold tassels step off that train?"

"Funny you should mention someone like that. A fellow of your description did step off and walk up and down the platform as if looking for someone. He paced until the whistle sounded to board, and he got back on. I wouldn't have paid any attention except for his insistent pacing."

"Looking for someone it appeared?" asks Chad.

"I think so. He kept glancing around as if expecting to see someone waiting here. He is someone of interest to you obviously."

"He is. If you see him again, let your sheriff know."

"Oh, lordy, are our passengers in danger?"

"Little late to worry about that now, friend. You're sure he got back on?"

"Oh, yes. He reboarded. He'll be in Hot Springs by now."

"That's what I'm hopin' for. Thank you."

Two sharp blasts from the engine's horn signal it's time to roll. Chad and Isaac step back aboard and slip into their coach. They don't see the man with the floppy hat.

"That man is not aboard, Chad."

"Not in this coach at least. Once we start movin', I'll go check out the other passenger coach. Let's sit down before we get knocked down."

They settle in their seat moments before the coach jerks forward. The engine yanks the line of railcars as it picks up speed.

Dolin was lookin' for someone or maybe a gang. Didn't find 'em. Is he just on the run or headin' this direction on purpose? What's waitin' for us in Hot Springs? Chad stares out the window as the scenery flashes past.

10

HOT SPRINGS

THE TRAIN COACH ROCKS AND ROLLS ITS WAY UP ONE steep ridge, over the crest, and down into another valley of the Ouachita Mountains. The railway is laid through thick forests and along rocky bluffs. The passenger coach is full to capacity. People are wearing all types of dresses, coats, shawls, bonnets, Stetsons, flat hats, flower and feather covered chapeaus, and everyone seems to be talking at the same time. The noise level even drowns out the constant clacking of the wheels on the rails.

In the last seat of the last row against the window, Rafe sits wrapped in his black duster.

Why didn't that Mex meet me in Fort Smith? He knew to meet me there. This job in Hot Springs is too big for me alone. Now, all these travelers climbed on at the Malvern Hill water stop. I ain't got enough bullets to kill all of them.

"Pardon me sir, are you from these parts?" The man beside Rafe in a black suit and bowler hat looks for a response. "I was asking because I'm from Memphis and going to Hot Springs for the waters. My wife feels they can help my constant back pains."

"Leave me alone." Rafe turns to the window.

"I didn't mean to intrude on your solitude. I've been talking with others on the train from St. Louis and Cincinnati who are doing as I am. I was only looking for some information about Hot Springs."

With a snarl, Rafe quicly pulls his Colt and shoves the end of the barrel against the traveler's chin. "I said, leave me alone."

Wide eyed, and turning pale, the Memphis man stutters. "Yesss...sirrr...I'll leave you alone." Quickly, the man jumps from his seat and walks to the front of the coach.

Rafe slowly rises, holsters his pistol, and walks out the coach door behind him to stand on the platform between the coaches. He smells the engine's smoke sweeping past. The train sounds a long low whistle as it climbs and descends another ridgeback approaching Hot Springs.

This is too big of a job for one person. Frank Flynn controls three gamblin' halls in Hot Springs, and there's enough money to be had for the takin', if planned out just right. I need the Mex and one more to make the job pay. I gotta get off this lunatic bin of a train. Rafe watches the trees whip past in front of him.

Chad walks slowly through the railroad coach attached to the one where he and Isaac are sitting. Their train left Eufaula a day behind the one carrying Rafe to Hot Springs. Near the Fort Smith water stop, Isaac felt a passenger in a black floppy hat and serape takes particular interest in the two of them. After reboarding and getting underway, Chad searches the two passenger coaches for the man.

Isaac waits for him on the platform between the two cars watching Chad move toward him.

"Any luck? Did you see him in there?" Isaac grips the handrails like an eagle grips a fish with its talons.

"Nope. Didn't see him. He's not in our coach or the other one. I didn't go through and check the livestock car. He might be there."

"How about in the mail coach?"

"Door's locked. Shouldn't be able to get in."

"What do we do now?"

"Wait."

"Wait for what?"

"If he's got a play to make, he'll show his hand. If not, we've got all worked up over nothin'."

"He was not paying attention to us for nothing. He is still on this train."

"That may be, but I can't check every corner. Malvern Hill is the next water stop before Hot Springs. I'll check the stock car then. In the meanwhile, let's get seated before we are tossed off this rockin' ride."

"All right, but I am watching just the same."

"Wouldn't think you'd do anything less."

Chad opens their coach's door and steps inside.

Nestled in the straw of a stall in the livestock car, Victor slowly runs his thumb over the blade edge of his Bowie knife.

I recognize the two men in the coach. They are the ones who shot at Rafe and me at the whiskey peddler's wagon. What are they doing on this train? I saw the big one flash a badge at the station agent in Fort Smith. A marshal? Trailin' Rafe, me, both? Ay, diablo, I will find a way to take care of them. Nobody shots at Gonzales without payin' a price. The smell of horses and straw mixed with the rocking motion and constant clacking of the wheels lull Victor to sleep.

"Malvern Hill, Malvern Hill water stop. Twenty minutes." The conductor shouts as he walks through the passenger car.

"Do we get off here?" Isaac strains to look ahead out of the window beside him.

"No. Keep your seat. I'm goin' to check out the stock car when we stop. It's just another water stop. Watch the depot for our mystery man. Don't go chasin' him yourself, just watch for him. I'll be back directly."

The train whistle sounds with a long wail to announce arrival into Malvern Hill. Chad is off the train before it comes to a complete stop. He walks rapidly alongside the platform and is waiting at the door of the stock car when the station helper opens it.

"You got stock in here, sir?"

"Yep. Two horses, a mule, and gear. Just want to check on them."

"I understand, I'd do the same." The helper rolls the door open. Chad steps into the car with his hand on his revolver. Glancing from left to right, he quickly surveys the area. Both Chad and Isaac's horses and the mule they picked up at Fort Smith are in their stalls, four goats are in a pen, six crates of chickens cackle noisily, a dozen cows low at being disturbed, an Appaloosa stands in an end stall with a blanket draped over its back, but Chad doesn't see a man. The roof hatch at the end of the car is open. He walks over to the ladder and looks upward briefly, then turns and leaves the car.

Isaac is relieved when he sees Chad enter the coach.

"Anything?"

"No. He might have been in the stock car but slipped out by climbing to the roof. You see anybody movin' along the platform?"

"I did not see our man. However, we've been invaded by travelers from many locations seeking transportation to Hot Springs. I heard people talking about being from St. Louis, Memphis, Cincinnati, Springfield, and Indianapolis. It seems the hot springs draw a crowd. They mentioned bath houses built along the main street."

"I'd heard about folks comin' to soak in the mineral waters."

"They are talking about communal bath houses."

"You mean y'all get in the bath together?"

"I believe that is what they are alluding to."

"Well, I never. Who's gonna climb in a bathtub with three or four other people?"

"We did it on the cattle drive with every river we crossed."

"What'd you mean?"

"All the cowboys took off their clothes and got in the water with the cattle."

"That ain't the same. They were workin'. Besides, they had their long johns on."

"Just the same. That is communal bathing."

"You know, this is just strange enough to check it out. We might have to take a look."

The train blasts two short whistles and jerks the coach forward as the engine builds up steam and momentum.

"Twenty miles to Hot Springs." Chad slides down in the seat and pulls his hat over his eyes. "Takin' a bath in a tub with three or four strangers. Well, I never."

"Are you just going to go to sleep?"

"Seemed like a good thing to do." Chad mutters from under his hat brim.

"What about that man?"

"Kinda figured you was gonna keep an eye out. Wake me before Hot Springs."

Huffing in frustration, Isaac watches the other occupants of the coach as they carry on with their animated conversations.

Chad and Isaac step from the train at the stone depot building in Hot Springs. Passengers leaving the coach rush past to claim baggage that is being unloaded and placed on carts. Friends and acquaintances of arriving passengers rush forward to greet them. Chad and Isaac bob and weave to avoid colliding with other people as they make their way to the stock car. Railroad personnel are leading the horses and other animals from the car. Chad hands the stockman the paperwork to claim their mounts, saddles, and gear. After walking their animals down the ramp at the end of the platform, Chad and Isaac saddle them, slip the bits on and buckle down the bridles, tie on their saddlebags, and slide the rifles into the scabbards. Chad loads the mule's pack as Isaac ties on bags and satchels carrying their gear and supplies. They step into their saddles and walk their horses down the road toward town.

Chad and Isaac ride past steep ridges that rise on both sides of the wide valley. Ahead, on one side of a large boulevard, they see six large buildings, three wooden structures, two brick, and one stone. On the other side of the roadway, a collection of single and multi-storied buildings are constructed from brick and wood. Most are hotels and gambling halls. Scattered up the hillsides are houses. At the far end of the valley and boulevard is a new stone construction of multiple stories. Carts, carriages, wagons, and men on horseback throng Main Street. Kerosene street lamps line both sides of the road and down the gardened island.

"This is the first honest boulevard I've seen since New York City. Wide roadways divided by the middle island of trees, grass, and flowers. It is gorgeous." Isaac stares in surprise.

"This place is crawling with people, construction, and business." Chad looks from left to right, trying to take in all the sights. "Let's ride down the street a ways and find us a hotel."

"I am following you." Isaac continues to be amazed at all the people busily going about their business.

Riding down the boulevard past the large buildings, they

quickly conclude these must be the bath houses. People are entering and leaving the structures. Carriages wait in front to pick up riders. Large windows open onto the boulevard, and people are seated under wide covered verandas. Waiters in starched white shirts and black trousers circulate through the crowd and serve their customers.

"If that is where y'all go to take baths, then I may reconsider." Chad points toward a large stone structure with wide arches, large windows, two stories tall, and shiny copper roofs with crenelated edges.

Crossing at an intersection, Chad leads Isaac toward a three-storied brick hotel flanked by a two-story gambling hall and a mercantile store. "Over there, let's give that place a go."

Approaching the hotel, two men wearing hotel jackets step toward them and grab the reins of their horses. The taller of the men steps between Chad and Isaac.

"Welcome to the Excelsior, gentlemen. We will see to your horses if you would care to step into the lobby."

Chad and Isaac dismount pull down their saddlebags and rifles and follow the second hotel man up the steps to the front doors. They are met by a bellman in hotel uniform and ushered into the building.

As they step through the glass paned, large, double doors, they are surrounded by soft piano music being played on a baby grand piano in the corner. The pianist acknowledges their entrance with a nod as he keeps playing.

In front of them, across the spacious lobby, is a long mahogany registration desk. Behind the desk is a back bar with a section of pigeon-hole cabinetry and expansive countertop space. Flower arrangements sit on the registration desk. Large pots of tall plants fill every corner and are strategically set around the lobby.

Through a framed opening on his left, Chad sees a library with stuffed chairs, a full wall of bookcases and books, and waiters moving from patron to patron taking drink orders.

Beside the library is another room where four tables have card games being played. Men hunch over their dealt hands, watch the dealer intently, and wager on the turn of each card.

Across the lobby, clusters of women are seated in deep conversations.

Overstuffed, tall-backed damask covered chairs are set in groupings and singly throughout the lobby. Sofas and chairs are arranged for easy conversations around the room.

Large paintings of Victorian landscape scenes adorn every wall.

To the right a framed opening leads to a dining room.

The wide staircase extends from the middle of the lobby to the second floor. Waiters travel up and down the stairs, carrying large silver trays with covered dishes, goblets, carafes, and bottles of liquor.

Messenger boys, in bellman uniforms, race through the lobby, calling people's names to deliver notes in envelopes.

Kerosene-lamped chandeliers hang from the high ceiling, and sconces are attached to the walls to provide additional lighting.

Chad slowly circles around, taking in the opulence.

"Isaac, this old boy has been to two county fairs and a church pie supper and never seen anything like this. It ain't no wonder folks are comin' here."

"My dear friend, this is New York City removed to the Ouachita Mountains of Arkansas. Welcome to the world I am familiar with." Isaac smiles at his friend's amazement.

"Welcome to the future, Marshal Westerman."

Chad adjusts his elbows on a table in the library, smoking a cigar and sipping his Kentucky bourbon. He dips the end of his cigar into the drink and then takes a long drag. He slowly exhales. Smoke forms a wreath around his head.

"Are you sure?" He looks at the waiter.

Isaac watches them both from across the table.

"Oh, yes, sir. There are twenty-four hotels in Hot Springs right now, and the large building under construction at the end of the boulevard is the new Arlington Hotel that will outshine anything already here."

"That, my friend, is hard to believe. Ain't it, Isaac?"

"Like you told me on the cattle drive, 'just wait and see.'" Isaac smiles.

"What about the hot springs?" Chad leans back in his chair.

"They are all-natural thermal waters that flow from forty-seven springs only on the western slope of Hot Springs Mountain."

"Only that mountain?"

"Yes, sir. Each bath house captures water from one or more springs and channels it into the building. There are individual bathing rooms inside, a communal pool, full bars with dining, and concierge service."

"What is 'conserge' service?" Chad furrows his eyebrows.

"Anything you want, sir. Anything you want." The waiter smiles.

"Well, I'll be whipped."

"That can be arranged." Isaac laughs out loud.

"Will that be all, sir?" The waiter starts to step away.

"Yes, thank you." Chad returns to looking out the windows at the bath houses across the boulevard. The waiter returns to the kitchen.

"So, how again do we find Dolin or the other man with the floppy hat in this place. Explain it to me really slow." Isaac leans forward, places his elbows on the table, and rests his chin in his hands.

"Well, it appears that it might be a tad more difficult than I might have mentioned."

"Really?" Isaac can't hide the sarcasm in his voice.

"All right, Mr. Marshal Wisenheimer, how do you propose we go about things?"

"Well, Marshal Westerman, I believe the more we move around, the more chance we have of passing each other in the crowds and not knowing it. I think it would be better to find a place, stay put, and wait for our killer to come to us."

"You mean stake out a spot, set the bait, and wait? Like we're catchin' polecats or some such?" says Chad.

"Certainly, not as I have said it, but, yes," replies Isaac.

"All right. Where?"

"While you were talking with the waiter, I was reading this handbill I picked up in the lobby. It looks like Frank Flynn runs the largest gambling establishment in town. He actually owns a few of them. I suggest we find a spot there and wait. Dolin will surely show himself."

"Let's do it tonight. No time like the present to get started. First, though, I want to walk over and take a look at that bath-house. I'm dying to see what it's like inside."

"Finish your cigar, we will take a look, and then go to Flynn's."

High up the hillside on Hot Springs Mountain, in a log cabin hidden from plain view, Rafe Dolin sits at a roughhewn timber table. Across from him sits Victor Gonzales. Two grimy glasses and an almost empty bottle of Old Grand Dad whiskey sits between them.

"Just how did you get away from those guys who shot at us?"

"*Amigo*, I am smarter than any *gringo*. I hide in the stock car while moving, and on the roof when the train stopped. It was simple."

"You ain't so dumb after all, Mex."

"*Me llamo es* Victor, not Mex."

"Victor, Mex, it won't make no difference after we take care of Flynn's place."

"*Si*, but it will take more than you and me, no?"

"I seen plenty of men running around this town. Find us a helper, somebody to be our lookout and not let us down. Think you can do that?"

"I will find someone. They will do as I say or die."

"Good, now go get it done. I gotta go see someone."

11

EVANGELINE

A YOUNG WOMAN GAZES OUT A SECOND STORY WINDOW watching the morning sun flood the main boulevard in Hot Springs. Light chases the shadows from doorways and alleys. She is slender with brunette hair that reaches mid-back and hangs in ringlets about her face. The ruffled pale blue chiffon robe she wears clings to her twenty-five-year-old voluptuous body, calling attention to every curve and swell. The silk fabric glistens. Her green eyes sparkle as light splashes through the window.

"Naomi, get out my blue dress," she commands a short, stooped Caddo Indian lady whose long black hair is pulled into two long pony tails on either side of her head.

"Yes, *Náttih Hakáayu'*, my white woman. Will you require a bonnet or hat for your outfit?"

"The matching blue bonnet will be fine. Now, hurry. Today is a busy one. Hurry."

"Yes, *Náttih*." The Indian lady rushes into the adjoining room.

The woman continues gazing through the window. *You've waited a long time to deal with Frank Flynn, Evangeline Bellefontaine. Now, is the time. My brother, as stupid as he is, finally arrived with his gang. Plans need to be made and executed quickly. Yes, executed, that's the right word.* She smiles as she goes into the adjacent dressing room.

Chad reclines on the padded seats of the open-topped barouche carriage as it rolls along the boulevard in Hot Springs. Isaac sits across from him. The driver flips his buggy whip over the backs of the two-horse team.

"You know, a man could get used to travelin' like this."

"This certainly is the more dignified way to ride. I do get tired of being horseback."

"Don't think this rig would last thirty minutes out on the trail, and our saddle horses serve us better out there."

"You will not convince me that the train and carriages will not soon take over."

"That may be, Isaac. That may be. Until then, your hind end is just gonna have to toughen up and fit the saddle."

The carriage stops in front of Hotel Excelsior. Chad opens the barouche door and steps onto the wooden sidewalk. Isaac is right behind him. They climb the steps into the lobby, walk to the library, and take their seats in two chairs by the front window.

"We've spent the better part of three days and nights at Flynn's place without seein' hide nor hair of Dolin. What if he's shyin' away from the biggest place and creepin' about the smaller gamblin' houses toward the end of town?" Chad motions for a waiter.

"It stands to reason that he might be doing that. We passed a smaller establishment that looked active when we arrived. I was especially taken by the name of the business…Evangeline's."

"Kind of has a nice ring to it, don't it?"

"I'm intrigued."

"Let's get a drink and then wander down to Evangeline's to take a look see."

"I could not have stated a better plan than that."

The office is a square room with pale green floral patterned flocked wallpapered walls. Stuffed sofas with decorative wood trim sit before three walls. A round leather ottoman rests in the middle of the room on a multicolored braided rug. Along the fourth wall sits a Chippendale writing desk with a leather covered, short backed swivel chair between it and the wall. Evangeline is at the desk writing rapidly, using a metal tipped pen and ink from an open jar on the desk. She pauses and reads to herself what she's written.

"There, it's done. Now, see that it's delivered." She folds the paper and hands it to Rafe.

Rafe leans forward in a straight-backed wooden chair in front of the table to retrieve the note.

"Why is she in here?" Rafe motions at Naomi, standing silently in the corner of the room behind Evangeline.

"She goes where I go. It's been that way since I found her in New Orleans. I saved her. She protects me. It's an Indian thing. Don't let her bother you. Of course, if anyone attempts to lay hands on me she will slice them crotch to Adam's apple in the blink of an eye."

"She ain't nothin' but a wrinkled old hag, and only seventy-five pounds soakin' wet."

"If you're brave enough, give her a go. I guarantee you'll regret it."

"Never mind her." Rafe glares at Naomi. The Indian's expression doesn't change. She wears a stone face. "I still don't see why you're inviting Flynn to a party. All we got to do is rob the bastard, clean him out, and shuck it out of here."

"Rafe, don't you ever get any smarter? You won't get out of the valley before Flynn has gunmen on you. I can't believe you've come with only one other man. I thought you had a gang."

"I did, but things have changed. By the time I got your telegram, I was down to one man. We can deal with Flynn."

"We've got to destroy him completely, not just take money from him."

"Why, why are you so hell-bent on destroyin' him?"

"You have no idea? Sometimes I'm not even sure you're my brother."

"Yeah, yeah. I've heard this before. When I left for the war, you and momma were alone in New Orleans. The Yankees took the city and made livin' miserable for y'all. Along comes a gambler named Flynn, and he takes care of you. You grow up. He takes advantage of you, uses you for his own pleasure, and blah, blah, blah. I've heard it all."

"Then you know that after the war, Flynn and I took to the riverboats, fleeced many a gambler, and made a pile of money."

"Well, I didn't ever see a penny of it. I was fightin' to stay alive in Texas."

"You were stealing cattle in Texas, running them to Abilene, and leaving a trail of dead bodies behind you."

"Makin' a livin', is makin' a livin'."

"That's what I'm doing, brother of mine. Making a living. Flynn beat me damn near to death in St. Louis when Naomi was away. He left me for dead, stole all our money, and slunk away. Naomi nursed me back to health and recovery. I found Flynn here in Hot Springs, followed him, and set up my business to take his away."

"Yeah, so you own and run a gamblin' house. So, what?"

"I thought I could run him out of business, I thought wrong. He's outfoxed me. His hired thugs keep his tables running wide open every night. I'm going to ruin him. It's revenge, brother. Pure and simple revenge."

"What's that got to do with me? Sounds like you've got all the baggage."

"You, dear brother, are my instrument of revenge."

"So, I'll walk into his place tonight and shoot the bastard. You have shuck of him then."

"Sometimes I'm not sure there's a brain in that hollow head of yours. I want to ruin the man, personally, financially, physically, emotionally, just like he did to me."

"Whoa, that's a lot of hate to carry, little sister."

"You don't know the half of it. I want his end to be slow,

painful, public, and complete."

"Evangeline, you ain't got to the point." Rafe shakes the paper in his hand.

"I'm inviting Frank Flynn here to talk about a social event for Hot Springs."

"A what?"

"A celebration for the town, one where he becomes the central figure of the event. Then, I can easily embarrass and ruin him."

"You're makin' this way too complicated. Generally, I just kill someone."

"Yes, I know. I've heard about you. Why do you kill like you do?"

"Just 'cause I like it."

"You are one sick, twisted person, brother, but I need you to help me right here, right now."

"We're both Dolin, although you're callin' yourself Bellefontaine. I'm here to help, if it ain't gonna take too long."

"Just as long as it takes to set up Flynn and drop him into hell."

Rafe laughs a maniacal outburst that sends shivers down Evangeline's back.

This sick fiend really is crazy. Whatever happened to my brother? I do believe he kills just because he likes to kill.

Chad and Isaac walk past the glass-paned wooden double doors and into Evangeline's gambling hall. The noise level is not as raucous as what they've experienced at Flynn's. There are still shouts of disgust and cheers over wins, but the overall countenance is more reserved. The hall is about one-half the size of Flynn's with a full complement of gaming tables—Faro, poker, black-jack. There are dice and roulette tables. Three spinning wheel positions. A bar of dark, almost black, mahogany stretches twenty feet along the back wall with a back bar surrounding a huge mirror.

The coziness and warmth of the hall comes largely from the furniture. The tables and chairs scattered around the open area are quality furnishings. The chairs are padded, the tables green felt covered. Flynn's place looks shabby in comparison to Evangeline's.

The six working girls' dresses are clean, and the women are well groomed. They proposition patrons and lead them to their cribs in the back of the building.

"This is some place, Isaac."

"It is much more distinctive than Mr. Flynn's, even if smaller."

"I wonder if an Evangeline owns it, or it's just the name."

"I believe the answer to your question is over there." Isaac points to a table at the end of the bar.

Beside an immaculately set table of glassware and china a beautiful woman stands. Chad is captivated by her brunette hair, gorgeous figure, and shocking blue dress.

"Think I'll go have a talk." Chad nods in the woman's direction.

"I will be singularly disappointed if you do not. I will find a spot at the bar." Isaac walks to get a drink.

Chad removes his hat and holds it in his hands as he nears the woman at the table.

"Good evening, ma'am."

"Good evening, cowboy."

The timbre and throatiness of her response catches Chad by surprise as does an old Indian woman in the shadows behind the woman.

"I'm lookin' for the proprietor. Might he be around?"

"Look no further, I'm the owner. Evangeline Bellefontaine."

"Chadbourne Westerman, ma'am. I'm pleased to make your acquaintance."

"My pleasure, cowboy. Would you care for a drink?" Evangeline points to a decanter sitting on the table.

A loud shout erupts from across the room. Arms wave around in the air. Men shove each other and shout back and forth.

"Looks like we have another winner at roulette." Evangeline sits down. "Be seated. It appears you came over here for conversation. I watched you when you came in."

"Yes ma'am. Thank you. I would like to ask some questions. By the way, is that a friend of yours?" Chad nods at Naomi.

Evangeline chuckles. "Don't worry about her. She's my constant companion. You'll never know she's there."

A bartender rushes over and places two clean glasses on the table.

"Thank you, Fred. Give my guest's friend free drinks. He's standing at the bar." She points at Isaac. The bartender nods and rushes back to serve patrons standing two deep along the bar.

"That's not necessary, ma'am, but appreciated."

"My pleasure, Chadbourne. Correct?"

"Yes, Deputy U.S. Marshal Chadbourne Westerman."

Her quick intake of breath is not lost on Chad. He watches

her sparkling green eyes dilate.

Somethin' ain't right. Does she run a crooked house? Is she hiding somethin'? Why the reaction?

"Marshal is it? What brings a U.S. Marshal to Hot Springs? We have lawmen aplenty in town already."

"I'm lookin' for a man."

"Oh, Marshal, I've been doing that for years." A weak smile wrinkles Evangeline's lips.

"I don't hardly believe you've had to look hard ma'am. You've probably got men lined up."

"You're too kind, Marshal. I don't think my male situation is what you're looking for though."

"No, ma'am. I'm lookin' for a stone-cold killer. A man who kills with no remorse."

"You think someone like that is here? In my establishment?"

"I ain't sure. I'd like your permission to sit kind of inconspicuous like for a couple of days and watch. Would you be willin' to allow me and my colleague to do that?"

"Certainly, Marshal. Please select the vantage point you'd like. May I ask who it is that you're seeking?"

"The outlaw's name is Dolin, ma'am. Rafe Dolin."

Evangeline's eyes twitch insignificantly at hearing her brother's name.

Damn, damn, damn that no good brother has dragged marshals to my doorstep just when I need to make my move against Flynn. I could kill him myself for doing this. I might just do it anyway. No, I've got to use him, got to warn him to keep away for a couple of days. Where was he hiding? Oh, yes, Buster's cabin on Hot Springs Mountain. I'll get word to him. This might slow me down, but I've waited too long for a lousy marshal or two to stop me.

"Is there anything else, Marshal? I need to get about my business."

"No ma'am. Thank you for accommodatin' us for the next few days." Chad rises from his chair and puts his hat on.

"Anything to assist the law, Marshal. My pleasure."

Evangeline watches Chad walk to the bar, tap Isaac on the shoulder, and both men walk around the hall looking for vantage points. She walks to the door behind the bar, opens it, and slips into her office. Naomi follows, quickly closing the door.

12

MEETING

Frank Flynn enters Parker's Bakery on Main Street and sees Evangeline sitting at the table beside the front window. His long brown hair is mussed by the breeze. The three-piece brown suit is freshly pressed and spotless. His white shirt is starched with creases that look sharp enough to cut. He carries a brown bowler hat in his hands as he walks toward her.

"Good afternoon, Miss Bellafontaine." He pulls a chair from the table and sits.

"We can dispense with the hypocrisy, Frank. You know me, and I know you. There are no secrets here."

"Very well, Evangeline. You've been a busy girl since your arrival, trying to undermine my business. It hasn't worked for you, has it?"

"No. You've managed to stymie me at every turn."

"Guess it shows who's the better gambler."

"It just shows who's able to purchase the most muscle, and you're surrounded by a bunch of thugs."

"Tch, tch, tch. Thugs is such a harsh word. I prefer business associates."

"I see. Ones that crack heads and break noses. You have quite a crew, Frank."

"I do try, my dear. I do try." He sits back with a malicious grin.

"I'm not here to talk about your business practices."

"Okay. What are we here for?"

"While I know we will never work together long term ever again—after all you did try to kill me—I think we can civilly cooperate."

"Pity you didn't just die in St. Louis. You've been a thorn gouging at me ever since."

Evangeline's pupils dilate as she glares at Flynn.

"The upcoming July fourth celebration in Hot Springs is bringing a flock of people into town. We can both waste our resources trying to drum up the most business separately, or we can host events that benefit both of us. I detest even bringing up the idea of working with you, but it is the best for business."

Why is this woman bringing me into a cooperative event? She knows our history, and yes, I did try to kill her in St. Louis. She can't be trusted. If I hadn't taken the money and run, she was planning to. Once a thief and liar, always a thief and liar.

"I may be interested. Tell me more." Flynn signals for the waitress to bring coffee and pastries to eat.

"The city is planning festivities for the Fourth of July, and between our two gambling houses we can add more activities. For example, sponsor a horse race with a cash prize, conduct special poker games with prizes, bring in entertainment from Little Rock, Memphis, or St. Louis."

"I can do all of that right now, why do I need you?"

"To share the risk of the cash prizes and to increase promotion for the events."

"All right. Let's say I agree, what's my take?"

"Fifty-fifty."

"I've got the larger operations. The share should be sixty-forty."

Evangeline glares at Flynn. Chokes back her anger and overwhelming desire to kill the man. She knows she must play the game in order to win in the end. *This sonofabitch is a snaky bastard, but I need to set him up and if that means giving him ground, then that's what I need to do. I can't be too easy doing it or he'll throw the hook.*

"If you're going to claim more, then you need more responsibility. You need to promote this to the town leadership as your idea and get their buy in."

"That's easily done. Most of them owe me money anyway." Flynn leans back in his chair as he studies Evangeline's face looking for giveaway signs that every gambler has. *I've got this tricky bitch now. Whatever she had up her sleeve, if I control things, I can take advantage of the activities and shut her down. This may just be the right move for me.*

"You lead the promotion, and your name is associated with the events we come up with. I'll do my part in funding and focus on supporting your lead. The split is sixty-forty. Agreed?" Evangeline smiles.

"This may just work out. I'll consider things and get back

with you." Flynn sits up straight in his chair.

"When?"

"Tomorrow. Now, if you'll excuse me, I've got real work to do. I hope you don't mind if I don't turn my back on you as I leave." Flynn rises from his chair and backs toward the door. Two men at the table beside the door stand and guard his departure.

The waitress arrives at the table and sits down her tray with cups, saucers, a coffee pot, and pastries.

Evangeline seethes inside. Hate consumes her as she continues to stare at Flynn's departure. She doesn't acknowledge the waitress's arrival.

"Will there be anything else, ma'am?"

Shocked back into reality, Evangeline replies, "No, no thank you. This will be all." The waitress walks away.

Evangeline continues her slow burn of revenge as she regains composure of her emotions. *I've got this low life now. He'll claim leadership of everything and it will all fail. The city will see him for the liar, schemer, and deceitful sack of shit he really is. That public humiliation is first. Next, I need to make sure Rafe is in a position to steal the prize money from the events and leave Flynn holding an empty bag. Finally, I'll arrange a way to separate Flynn from his guards and then have Rafe beat him within an inch of his life. Knowing Rafe, he'll want to go too far. I want Flynn beaten and broken but still barely alive, so he'll have to climb back through the pain just like I did.*

Evangeline stands, drops money on the table to pay for the coffee and pastries. Looking around the bakery, she acknowledges nods from patrons of her gambling hall. She walks out into the sunlight.

The kerosene lamps cast eerie shadows on the office walls. Darkness is outside the windows. Evangeline sits at her desk, and Rafe lounges in the straight-backed chair across from her.

"So, Flynn took the bait?"

"Like a dumb catfish. He took a day to consider my proposition, but he bought the idea. Now, we go to work."

"Good. When do I kill him? I've been itchin' to since I got here."

"Listen to me, my sick-in-the-head brother. You are not killing Flynn. Yes, you'll steal every dime he has and beat him beyond sensibility, but you'll leave him barely alive. Do you understand?"

"Yeah, yeah. I understand, and I'm gettin' real tired of you callin' me names and such. I came here to help you because you asked. I got things that need tendin' to in the Territory."

"You came here because you saw a chance to steal money and kill some fool. You're not kidding me one instant. I'll give you the chance to do the first and almost complete the second. We have an agreement?"

"Okay, sis. We'll do it your way. I don't like it, but I'll do it."

"Good. Now get out of town and stay out until I send for you. That U.S. Marshal has been staking out this place waiting to see you. My impression of him is that he's like a bulldog. He isn't going to turn loose."

"Maybe I can kill him. That would satisfy my havin' to leave Flynn barely alive."

"What you do with the marshal is not my concern after you

complete our agreement."

"Good, now that's somethin' I can sink my teeth into. Somebody dies." Rafe stands, opens the office door leading outside, and slips into the darkness. He quietly shuts the door behind him.

Midway along the front wall in Evangeline's Gambling Hall, Chad looks across the room and sees Isaac against the far wall. Isaac's head is down, and it appears he's sleeping. Evangeline enters through the office door beside the bar with Naomi behind her. She walks toward Chad. He removes his hat as he gets to his feet.

"Evenin' Miss Evangeline. Didn't expect to see you here so late."

"Marshal, it's my house. I never leave it."

"You live here?"

"Oh, yes. I've an apartment on the second floor. It's not overly large, but it is comfy for me. Having any luck?"

"No, ma'am. It's been three days, and we've not seen anyone who looks like Dolin. May have to relocate to another establishment and keep lookin'."

"You're welcome to stay here as long as you like, but if you are not getting results, maybe your man will turn up at another location."

"We'll wrap up tonight, Miss Evangeline, and leave. Thank you for allowin' us to use your hall."

"My pleasure, Marshal. I want to cooperate with the law."

Evangeline walks toward the roulette tables leaving Chad standing beside his chair.

You just keep looking to your hearts content marshal. I think I'll use you to help me ruin Flynn. What better way to discredit him than having him accused and arrested for murder. If I can arrange things, I'll be able to tie up loose ends, frame Flynn, and walk away with a fortune. Oh, Evangeline, you are one clever girl.

A wide smile creases her face as she approaches the gambling tables.

13

NEXT STEPS

THE MORNING SUN STREAMS THROUGH THE FRONT windows of the library at Hotel Excelsior. Chad lets the sunshine beat down on him as he sits in an overstuffed Queen Anne chair. His hat is pulled forward over his eyes, his chin rests on his chest, and his breathing is deep.

"You look like a cat soaking up sunshine, Chadbourne." Isaac, sitting nearby, shuffles through the pages of the newspaper he holds upright in front of him.

"I'm sleepin', don't bother me."

"I have never known you to really sleep. You are always alert."

"Now that you woke me up, what do you want?"

"I have been elucidating myself with the content from the local Hot Springs Gazette."

"I hope you can take shots for that elucidatin'."

"Never mind that. It appears that Frank Flynn has more money than King Midas."

"He does regularly shear those sheep that wander into his gamblin' houses."

"He is spending it righteously as well. The article in the paper says he is hiring every available man to construct a horse racing track."

"A what?" Chad straightens up in the chair and shoves his hat back on his head.

"A race track. It seems he has convinced the city fathers that in order for Hot Springs to grow, it needs a race track. Just yesterday, a beer drummer from St. Louis was telling me about a very successful track constructed in Louisville, Kentucky. The Louisville Jockey Club owned by Meriwether Lewis Clark, Jr."

"Where's Flynn gonna build this track?"

"He owns the large meadow on the west end of town and he has two draft horse teams leveling a track using road graders. His men are building grandstands and a club house. He claims it will be ready for the July fourth celebrations in a little over one month from now."

"Why? Does he want Hot Springs to be like Louisville?"

"Civic minded, maybe?"

"From what I've seen, Flynn ain't civic minded unless there is something in it for him."

"It is horse racing. That is gambling, so Flynn is interested."

"There's also a lot of risk involved, and I think Flynn only likes sure bets."

"Another article says that he is making space in his largest gambling hall to host a high-stakes poker game during the holiday."

"That's right down his alley. How high are the stakes?"

"The newspaper says the buy-in is five thousand dollars per person."

"Whew. That's some buy-in. That's gonna limit the players, but those who come are totin' some big money."

"This should draw in gamblers from distant locales. I would imagine New Orleans, Memphis, Cincinnati, and St. Louis to name a few."

"Could be even farther away than that. It's gonna draw outlaws too. He's buildin' up to somethin', and I think we need to do a little diggin' into it."

"He has done nothing illegal. Why is it our business?" Isaac looks shocked.

"Nothin' we can see, but where there is smoke, there's bound to be a fire. Besides we ain't doin' nothin' else."

"Aside from your homespun sayings, I do agree with your statement of our current state of lackadaisicalness."

"What? Sometimes you just say things to confuse me. I did wire Judge Parker the other day about Dolin's trail goin' cold. He sent a message back sayin' he's not heard anything about him either and would like us to stay put for a while."

"There are, most assuredly, worse places to stay than here."

"That's for certain, though we're burnin' through our bankroll kind of quick. We can probably stay for another couple of months or three."

"So, in the meanwhile you are recommending that we investigate Frank Flynn's sudden turn toward civic worthiness?"

"Yep. Somethin' doesn't add up and deserves takin' a look at."

"Maybe we will find Dolin in the midst of all the activities."

"Sounds like somethin' he wouldn't want to miss. Let's go

take a look at that race track Flynn's buildin'."

"Lead on, Marshal Westerman." Chad and Isaac stand and walk out of the hotel.

The buggy is pulled to the side of the road. The horse nibbles at grasses. Rafe's right foot rests on the running board. He holds the reins of his horse while Evangeline leans forward in the seat to talk.

"Flynn has taken the bait. He's investing heavily in the race track and poker game. Once the grandstands and club house are built, you'll burn them down. When the buy-in money is collected for the poker game, you'll steal it. Any questions?"

"Well, sure. How do I get into the gamblin' house to get the money? Anybody guardin' the race track? I can't just waltz up there with coal oil and not expect trouble."

"You work out the details. That's why you're getting to keep the money you rob. All I want is to see Flynn ruined. Finally, you'll need to beat Flynn."

"About that, he's always got guards around him. How am I supposed to get him alone?"

"Leave those arrangements to me. I'll let you know when it's time."

"Me and Victor are gettin' kind of antsy waitin' out here in the woods. We're gonna head into town tonight."

"You know the marshals are still in town, right? If you get caught, I'll kill you myself. I don't want you spoiling all that I've set in motion. Do you understand me?"

"Yeah, yeah, I hear you, but keepin' Victor cooped up ain't gonna get it. We'll be right careful."

"Rafe, if you mess me up, you'll live hard."

Rafe steps into his saddle and rides away.

Evangeline watches his departure.

I've waited years for my revenge and no stupid brother of mine is going to destroy this opportunity. Besides, he's a loose end, and loose ends have a way of being chopped off.

She yanks the reins on her horse and turns the buggy around, heading for town.

The building in the meadow has been framed and men are scrambling around putting the roof on the structure. Twenty yards away, a larger wooden building rises up beside a graded race track. Workers are busily installing gradated rows of bench seating. Chad and Isaac maneuver their horses through scurrying men, wagons, and piles of building materials as they approach the grandstand.

"There's Flynn standing on the top row." Chad points toward the stands.

"He looks like he is directing everything from up there." Isaac stops, dismounts, and ties his horse to a stack of lumber.

"Let's see if we can attract his attention and get him to come down. Those seats, and as a matter of fact, this whole structure don't look all that steady." Chad dismounts.

"Looks like he is coming down right now."

"Flynn, Flynn, you got a minute?"

Frank Flynn carefully steps his way through the construction debris as he approaches Chad.

"Well, well, Marshals. To what do I owe this visit?" Flynn leans against a pile of boards.

"Heard about your venture and wanted to see what's happenin."

"This is it." Flynn waves his arms around. "A one and one-quarter mile horse race track, grandstand, stables, and club house."

"You've got men out here like ants on an ant hill."

"Got to. I'm aimin' to have this open and operating for the July fourth celebrations. I've already contacted some horse breeders about bringing their quarter horses in to race."

"You mean this ain't just for anybody to show up and race their horse?"

"Oh, hell, Marshal. This racing business is professional stuff. Big money and special horses. It ain't for your hell-and-gone cowboys. I'm arranging with the railroad to sponsor rail coaches to bring spectators and gamblers for this event from all the major cities around Hot Springs."

"You're sinkin' a slug of money into this venture, Flynn."

"Like they say, Marshal. You got to spend money to make money."

"You're just as likely to attract an element of persons you don't want to have around."

"If you're talkin' about thieves, robbers, and such, I live with them right now and manage just fine. My boys take care of business. I don't intend to let it hinder me now."

"You've got your work cut out for you to have everything up and running by July fourth. I know you're fixin' to make more money with all of this, but why did you jump on it now?"

"An acquaintance of ours, Evangeline Bellefontaine, happened to mention something about this in a passing conversation. I looked into it and determined to do something before someone else did."

"So, there is a sense of civic duty behind your activities?" Isaac watches Flynn for a response.

"Hell no, Marshal. It's money. Plain and simple. Money. Now, if you men will excuse me, I've got workmen to oversee." Flynn walks toward a group of men raising wall beams.

"There you go, Isaac. Money. Plain and simple."

"Greed. Avarice. Mankind is doomed."

"Maybe so, Isaac. Maybe so." Chad steps into his saddle and turns his horse toward town.

Why would Bellefontaine be in cahoots with Flynn? I thought they were at each other's throats. If there's money to be made, why'd she give it up. Somethin' just don't stack up. I wonder if the Judge knows anything about Flynn or Bellefontaine. Might be worth a telegram to find out.

14

SIGHTING

DAYLIGHT DIMS AS EVENING SHADOWS CREEP ACROSS the valley between the mountains that surround Hot Springs. Two men sit at a table on the veranda of The Buckhorn Bath House watching the lamplighter carry out his job of igniting the kerosene street lamps along the main street. A waiter places cups of steaming coffee on the table.

"It has been chewin' at me since we left Flynn," Chad says.

"What has been chewing at you?" Isaac reaches for his coffee.

"Why would Bellefontaine tell Flynn about a gold mine in horse racing?"

"Maybe she is wanting to get into his good graces."

"That man's got no good graces. In dealin' with people, there's aways an angle. You gotta look for the greed, lust, or power."

"Did pushing cattle or becoming a marshal turn you into a cynic?"

"Don't know about bein' cynical. Just know that people are people, and there's somethin' afoot."

"Okay, let us say you are correct. What would induce this action by Bellefountaine?"

"Didn't you go to the newspaper office yesterday to check on Flynn and Bellafontaine?"

"You know I did." Isaac pulls a page of paper from his jacket pocket and lays it on the table straightening it out. "I have my notes right here."

"What did you find?"

"From past copies of the newspaper I found numerous articles. Early on, it seems that Flynn arrived in Hot Springs at least a year prior to Bellefontaine."

"And?" Chad leans forward, his interest peaked.

"An article stated that they are both from St. Louis and worked the riverboats. One column said Bellefontaine opened her gambling house to go one better than Flynn and put him out of business."

"Well, that ain't workin'. What else?" Chad picks up his coffee and takes a drink.

"Interestingly, I found a bit of information buried deep in another article."

"And? Don't just sit there keepin' it in."

"Evangeline's name has not always been Bellefontaine."

"Really? What was it?"

"Dolin."

"Ain't that a tidy coincidence?"

"Dolin is a common enough name. Back in Five Points on Long Island in New York, Murphy, Dolin, O'Rourke, and

O'Connor are all common names."

"This ain't New York, Isaac, and the Dolin name sticks out like a busted thumb."

"You think they are related?"

"Can't say for sure, but I've got my suspicions. This takes some lookin' into. Still, I'm questionin' why the small rat would try to do in the big rat. What's the bait?"

"You are talking in metaphors that I am unable to follow."

"Think about it, Isaac. Why would Evangeline feed a gold mine in horse racing to Flynn if she's tryin' to take him down? It don't make sense."

"Since you have stated it that way, is it inconceivable that she could possibly set him up and then plan to pull the rug from under him, so to speak?"

Chad slams his open hand down on the table rattling the cups and spilling coffee. "Precisely, my dear Isaac. Precisely."

"I'm not certain if I am more shocked at your selection of proper English words or your using them correctly."

"Well, pardner, even an ol' dog has new tricks. We been watchin' the wrong side of the gamblin' house. Our Dolin ain't comin' in the front door, he's slinkin' in the back."

"That might certainly be the case if both individuals we are discussing are related, near or distant."

"I'm bettin' you a dollar to a dime they are related. Now, who gains from them both bein' here? Rafe Dolin is probably chasing the money, and Evangeline is after the money as well? No, she's got money. What's drivin' her? Power? Lust? Ain't got that figured out yet."

"Supposing your suppositions are correct, what is our next step?" Isaac leans forward anticipating Chad's response.

"We go and watch them. First, to confirm I'm right on them

being connected, and then to figure out what's goin' on."

"Why do I feel like we have never left being range detectives?"

"Well, marshalin' does take the same skills. Let's go."

The alley behind Evangeline's Gambling Hall is as dark as the insides of a well. Chad and Isaac stand inside a stall of the stables behind the hall. A single horse shares the livery with them. It quietly flicks its tail. Light twinkles from two back windows of the building they watch.

"You think Dolin will show?" Isaac shuffles his feet for more comfort.

"Maybe tonight, maybe tomorrow."

"How will you know it is Dolin? I cannot hardy see my hand in front of my face."

"He has to go in the backdoor between the windows. When it opens, we'll have light."

"Then what? Do we rush him?"

"Only if you want to get killed. No, once he's inside, you'll go around and enter from the front and I'll go in the back."

"What if he is not alone?"

"We'll cross that bridge when we get there. Do you have any more 'what ifs' you want to ask? I'd like to pay attention to what's movin' around outside."

"You see someone coming?"

"Shhhhhh…get down."

"What if…?"

"Shut up."

The steady clopping of an approaching horse sounds in the alley. Chad can barely see a man on horseback carefully weaving his way through the alley. He watches him pause at every loud outburst of noise from gambling houses to make certain he's not discovered. At Evangeline's, the rider dismounts, and ties his horse to a post. Moving to the back door, he knocks three times, stops, and knocks three more times. The door cracks open. Chad leans forward to get a good look.

"Is it him? Is it Dolin?" Isaac whispers as he moves to get a better view. He kicks an empty can sitting beside him in the stall. It rattles and bangs against the wooden walls.

The horseman races to his mount, flings himself into his saddle, and digs in his spurs. The horse bolts down the alley, galloping past the stable doorway. Chad races to the open doors just in time to see a duster coat flapping like a flag behind the man disappearing from view.

"Well, that just does it. What were you doin'?" Chad turns to face Isaac.

"I just took a step or two. Did not see the can. Was it Dolin?"

"Can't say it was or wasn't. Didn't get a good look. Only saw a duster."

"Will he come back?"

"Would you? He knows someone's watchin' the back. Ain't likely."

Walking into the alley and away from Evangeline's, the men move to Main Street.

"You smell like kerosene, Isaac. Did you spill some on yourself?"

"Of course not. You have been with me. When would I have had the opportunity to be around kerosene?"

"Don't know. What was in the can you kicked in the stable?"

"How would I know? It is black as pitch in that stall. All I know is that it was there, and I stumbled into it."

"Why would anyone keep kerosene in a stable? Don't make good sense."

"It may not, but what do we do now?" asks Isaac.

"In the morning, I'm telegraphing Judge Parker to let him know it's possible, just possible, Dolin is still here. Then I'm getting a special made pair of hobbles for you."

"It was an accident. It was dark, and I did not see that can. I am sorry."

"Sorry, don't get it. Hobbles will." Chad smiles knowing Isaac can't see his face in the darkness.

A single candle burns on the rickety wooden table. Rafe paces the small cabin's only room. Victor sits at the table and pours the last of the whiskey into a grimy glass.

"There was somebody waitin' for me tonight." Rafe continues pacing back and forth across the room.

"Who was waiting, amigo?" Victor scratches his beard stubble and drinks the whiskey.

"Don't know who. Bet it was that marshal fella."

"Why would it be the marshal. He does not know we are here."

"Maybe that crazy sister of mine told him."

"Why would she? She wants us to do a job for her, no?"

"Yeah, yeah, she wants us to do the dirty work for her. What if we just go into town, rob Flynn, and ride on?"

"*Si, amigo.* We can do that, but then we have Flynn's men, the marshals, and your sister chasing us. We only keep adding to those who want to kill us."

"All right, all right. You go to town and tell my sister to meet me on the road where she did last time. I need to get to the bottom of this before we go on."

"*Si,* I go." Victor walks to the door. He looks over his shoulder. "I will also ask her when we get to kill somebodies. I'm tired of waiting."

"Go on, you knife-lovin' Mex. Give my sister the message and get back here. Don't bring nobody with you. You *comprende*?"

"*Si,* I will be back. If a marshal gets in my way, he dies."

Evangeline rushes from the gambling hall to the office doorway behind the bar where Naomi is waiting.

"Mistress, it is the bandito with message from your brother." Naomi gestures to the office.

"You didn't leave him standing in my office, did you?"

"No. He is outside back door."

"Good, I'll talk to him there." Evangeline sweeps past Naomi. She opens the door a crack, places her foot against the bottom, and leans forward.

"What do you want?"

"Rafe, he sends me. Who was watching the back of the building?"

"What? What are you talking about?"

"Rafe, he comes earlier, hears noise from stables, someone watches your backdoor."

"There's no one staying in the stables."

"*Si, señorita*. Rafe, he says someone was there. It is true, no?"

"I have no idea. Wait. It could be the marshal. He's been in watching the front of the building for a few days. Maybe he figured to watch the back for a while. Yes. That's it. It was the marshal…Marshal Westerman."

"Where can I find this Marshal Westerman, señorita?"

"Why?"

"It is time to do something about his being alive, I think."

"No. No, don't bother him. I have plans to use him."

"When do we get to take Flynn's money?"

"Soon. Very soon. The race track is almost ready and the participants for the high-stakes poker game are arriving every day. Stay out of town. Tell Rafe I'll meet him on the road, same place as before, in two days. I'll lay out the plan then."

"*Dos dias*, two days, *señorita*. No more. Your brother will be there. *Buenos noches*."

Evangeline quietly closes the door and leans back against it.

He'd as soon kill me as talk to me. I don't trust that man. His eyes say he is a blood thirsty killer. Rafe has to part ways with him before it's too late.

Naomi watches Evangeline's face.

"I can end it with him, mistress." Naomi uncrosses her arms and pulls a slender stiletto from a hidden sheath up her dress sleeve.

"I know you can and have used your knife for me in the past, but not just yet. We need this scum to do what needs to be done. I've come too close to have someone like him mess things up."

"Very well, mistress. You let me know when." Naomi slides the knife back into its sheath.

"I need to keep everything running smoothly." Evangeline walks from the office back into the gambling hall. Naomi follows, closing the office door.

The morning newspaper lies on the table in the dining room of the Excelsior Hotel. Chad and Isaac are finishing the last morsels of pancakes from their breakfast.

"Are you going to tell me about the telegram that was just delivered to you?" Isaac pushes his chair back from the table.

"Maybe. I just scanned it. Give me a minute to reread it."

"I know you went out earlier, and I am assuming you sent a message to Judge Parker. Is this his response?"

"Yep." Chad continues to reread the telegram. "Well, well, well. We've got ourselves into a real sticker patch." He hands the message to Isaac.

Eagerly, reading the telegram, Isaac pauses.

"You think this is the same person?"

"Judge Parker thinks it could be, and that's good enough for me."

"He says there is an outstanding warrant in St. Louis."

"Yep."

"For knifing and killing."

"Yep."

"They are associated with Evangeline Dolin."

"So, he says."

"There are politicians who have been killed by Evangeline because they owed her money. That's a pretty good motive."

"You can't kill politicians and not expect the law to take notice."

"What are we supposed to do?" asks Isaac.

"You didn't see anything in the message about actions to take, did you?"

"No, I did not."

"Then, the Judge is leaving it up to us?"

"All right, then what do we do?"

"Nothin' just yet. We wait."

"Wait? What for? Someone else to die?"

"Maybe. Maybe. Just hope it ain't us."

15

HIGH STAKES

THE BUGGY SITS BESIDE THE ROAD LEADING UP HOT Springs Mountain. It's been parked for over thirty minutes. The horse fidgets and swishes its tail impatiently. Evangeline watches two men slowly ride down the road toward her.

"It's about time you got here." Evangeline is agitated, and her voice betrays her impatience.

"Yeah. We been waitin' and watchin' to make sure nobody followed you. If that marshal is on to us, we can't be too careful."

"All right. Well, you're here now."

The two horsemen ride up close to the buggy.

Rafe crosses his arms and leans on his saddle horn. "We need to know the plan, and we need to know it now. The marshals are makin' it too hot to hang around, and, with no plan, Victor and I are going to clean out Flynn and head for the Territory."

"You'll go when I say you'll go and not before." Evangeline glares at her brother. "I've worked too hard to get to this point for you and that Mex to mess things up." Her hand slides under the blanket covering her lap touching the Colt revolver on the seat beside her.

Victor smiles a reptilian grin. "*Señorita*, your *hermano* just wants to know what you plan. You can share that, no?"

Shivering at Victor's grin, Evangeline looks at Rafe. "Flynn has been bringing in horses, trainers, and big money gamblers for the past week. The high stakes poker games start tonight, and the races begin first of next week."

"Good. Go on. When do we do somethin'?" Rafe straightens in his saddle.

"The stake money has been collected for the poker games, and Flynn has it in a safe in his office."

"Yeah, and he has a squad of thugs guarding it around the clock, I bet."

"He does have it guarded, so we need a diversion to move them away."

"What kind of diversion?"

"You and him," Evangeline points at Victor, "will burn the race track grandstand."

"Burn the place? To the ground?"

"Every wooden stick of it. Burn it all, everything."

"*Amigo,* your *hermana*, she is one scary *chica*." Victor pushes his flat hat back on his head.

"You're right, Victor, and she's dead set on this happenin.'"

"I've purchased cans of coal oil to use. They are stored in the stable behind my gambling hall. Take them and saturate the race track building. Start the fire and get back to town. When the alarm is shouted about the fire, Flynn will pull everyone he's got to fight the fire. That will leave the office lightly guarded. You should be able to take care of whoever is left, blow the safe, and get out of Hot Springs in the confusion."

"Blow up the safe. With what?"

"With the dynamite I purchased. It's in the stable as well."

"Anything you didn't think of?"

"You wanted my plan, now you have it. Can you make it happen?"

"Victor and I can do what you're askin'. Where will you be?"

"Close to Flynn."

"Why?"

"Because I'm bringing him to you to finish the plan."

"And that is?"

"Beat him bad. So bad it almost, and I said almost, kills him. I want him to hurt like I hurt when he beat me. Break his arms, legs, anything to cripple him, but don't kill him. Do you understand?"

"Where will you bring him?"

"To the stock car on the train at the depot."

"Why the train?"

"It's the fastest way out of Hot Springs. On horseback, Flynn's guards will catch up. On the train we can be miles away and leave Flynn for dead in the railcar before anyone is the wiser."

"*Amigo*, she has a plan, no?" Victor's voice reflects his respect for Evangeline's plot.

Chad and Isaac walk down the steps in front of Hotel Excelsior and onto the wooden sidewalk. They turn toward the café a block away.

"I don't know if I'll ever get used to cookin' for myself again," says Chad.

"The cuisine is much better here in Hot Springs. I have to admit that your constant diet of *frijoles* and beef does get old."

"Yeah, but it sticks to your ribs."

"That has never been an appropriately appetizing euphemism that I've gotten used to."

"A eupha..who."

"Never mind. What are we going to do about the Dolins?"

"We are goin' to take another look at the stables this morning. Kerosene in a haystack like that stable don't cotton to no good in my books. We'll check it out."

"If you mean we will go uninvited, does that mean we trespass?"

"What do you think we did last night?"

"Oh. Well, yes, I see. All right, we'll go investigate."

"Couldn't have said it better." Chad walks into the café as Isaac follows.

A light mist covers the buildings and ground as low-lying clouds drift through the valley of Hot Springs. The water droplets twinkle crystal-like in the pale sunlight. Chad slips into the stable behind Evangeline's Gambling Hall.

"Isaac, take a look under that tarp-covered stack in the

fourth stall. I'll check out the other pile across from it."

Pulling back the cloth, Isaac turns to Chad. "It's a bunch of cans of kerosene."

"Same over here, along with a box of dynamite and blastin' caps."

"Why would someone need all this kerosene and dynamite?"

"To make a big fire and a loud bang."

"Where?"

"That's the question, Isaac. Where for sure."

"You do not suppose it is for some common purpose or normal usage, do you?"

"Not likely. Not this much. I'd be hard pressed to see anythin' but trouble tied to this stash."

"We've come and seen this. Should we go before we are seen?"

"Yep. Cover it back up like you found it, and let's get out of here."

Chad and Isaac straighten the tarps over the kerosene cans and quickly leave the stables.

At the window of the gambling hall across the ally, Naomi quietly stands watching the men depart.

The marshals know too much. They snoop too much. It is time they know nothing ever again. I will tell the mistress and take care of both of them.

Evangeline sits at her table in the gambling hall watching customers belly up to the bar and risk their money at the gambling tables. Naomi enters from the office and leans over Evangeline's shoulder to whisper in her ear.

"Both of them in the stables?" Evangeline looks at Naomi.

"Yes. Both marshals."

"This make things more difficult. I'll have to accelerate the plan. Get word to Rafe to pick up the kerosene tonight and start the fire. Everything goes tonight. Go. Get word to him."

"Yes, mistress. Would you like me to take care of the marshals?"

"You are so good at that, yes. Make sure they don't bother us again."

"Very well. It is done."

"Now, go. We've got things to do." Evangeline walks toward the office. As she steps behind the bar, she reaches underneath and picks up a lead-filled black jack from the shelf, slips it into her handbag, and continues through the office doorway. Naomi follows and closes the door.

16

HOT TIMES

TWO MEN LOAD ALL THE KEROSENE CANS INTO Evangeline's buggy emptying the stable. The dynamite is taken from the box and placed in saddlebags, and the blasting caps are carefully folded up in cloth rags and slipped into a shoulder pouch.

"That's all of the coal oil?" Rafe takes one last look around.

"*Si, amigo*. It is all in the buggy."

"Okay, lets hitch up the horse and lead him out of town real easy like. Sun will be goin' down in an hour, so we should be able to light up the sky tonight."

"*Bueno, bueno*. It will be a fire like nothing before, no?"

"It's bound to be a real big blaze. Let's get goin'." Rafe leads Evangeline's horse around and backs it into the buggy shafts and begins harnessing.

"What if some mens guard the race track?"

"We kill 'em."

"It has been a while. I may be slow in killing *el hombre*." A sinister grin creeps across Victor's face."

"Well, don't take too long. We got work to do and a fire to start."

Rafe steps into his saddle, picks up the buggy horse's halter rope, and leads the loaded wagon out into the alley.

Evening slips quietly into the Hot Springs valley.

Two mounted men and the horse-led buggy move quietly toward the west end of the valley.

"Are we heading for the opening of the high stakes poker games?" Isaac rushes to keep up with Chad as he walks from the Excelsior Hotel toward Flynn's Gambling Hall.

"Yep. I want to see who all the players are, and it appears the whole town is turning out for the event."

"Look at the line of buggies and carriages in front of Flynn's."

Isaac watches as wagon after wagon unloads passengers. The crowd walking the sidewalk becomes more congested and starts backing up the closer Isaac and Chad get to the steps. People shuffle, jostle, and some push to keep in line as they approach the wide-open double glass paneled doors.

Suddenly, Isaac shouts out in alarm.

"Quit jabbing me." He twists around, and his jacket wraps around a blade poking him. A slim stiletto clatters to the sidewalk.

Isaac is face to face with Naomi.

"What are you shouting about?" Chad turns and sees Naomi reach up her sleeve and pull out another stiletto.

She jabs it toward Chad.

He slaps her arm away and pulls his Colt.

Naomi makes a feinting move to the left and slashes to the right.

Chad steps back, levels his gun, and triggers two quick shots.

Screams and shouting erupt from the crowd, and people panic to get away from the gunfire. Men and women run into, around, and against Isaac. He takes five steps back.

The crowd keeps its distance but forms a circle around Chad.

Naomi's body lies on the sidewalk.

"That is, that is Miss Evangeline's woman, Naomi," Isaac sputters in shock. "Why would she pull a knife on you?"

"Check your back and side, Isaac. You were her first target."

Isaac pulls his jacket around to find a large slice along the back. The side of his vest is cut as well. Only a fraction of an inch kept the blade from piercing his side. His face turns ashen.

"She tried to kill me."

"Yep. She almost did or at least made a good stab at it."

"Why? Why would she want to kill me?"

"Because you're a marshal if for no other reason."

"This is what she did in St. Louis for Miss Evangeline?"

"I would imagine so, Isaac. Only here she made a big mistake."

"What mistake? She almost killed me and sliced you up."

"No. She brought a knife to a gun fight. Big mistake."

Naomi's body is crumpled in a heap on the ground. Chad uses his foot to push her onto her back and finds two large black powder burn holes in the middle of her chest.

"I don't believe she'll be pullin' a knife on anybody again." Chad holsters his Colt.

Two sheriff's deputies maneuver their way through the crowd and stand in front of Chad.

"What happened, Marshal?" The taller of the two carries a shotgun.

"That woman attempted to kill both Marshal Wisenheimer and myself. You'll need to get the mortician."

"The Sheriff will need to hear the whole story." The shorter deputy kneels to check over Naomi's body.

"Tell the Sheriff I'll be along directly. First, I'm goin' into Flynn's to see what is happening there."

"You can tell him there. He's in the hall by the front door. We have deputies covering every door and window in the place."

"Sounds like you're expecting a lot of trouble."

"You just saw some. We're expecting every strong arm, pickpocket, and scum to crawl out of their holes and take advantage of the townsfolk attending this affair."

People continue to move around Chad, Isaac, and the deputies. All gawk at Naomi's body.

"Deputy, get a blanket and cover her until the mortician can get here. No sense in keeping the body on display."

"I'll take care of it, Marshal. You make sure to see the Sheriff."

"I will. Come on, Isaac. Wear your rags into the gala."

"A perfectly good suit ruined. I've kept this suit for a while with no damage, and dang, that woman cuts it to shreds."

"Better the suit than you, my friend. Better the suit."

"Indeed."

Chad and Isaac reach the doorway and muscle their way through the crowd jamming the opening. Women wearing long dresses. Men in top hats and tails. Every type of clothing of every description covers the noisy, shouting crowd. Everyone clamors to get into the gambling hall.

Breaking through the mob, Chad and Isaac are passed into the building by Flynn's guards who keep the crowd at bay.

"What have they done in here?" Isaac looks around in amazement.

The gambling hall has been transformed.

Sconces on the walls sparkle with brass reflectors, splashing kerosene lamp light into the open area. Huge coal oil-lamped chandeliers suspend from the high ceiling.

In the open area, all the tables and chairs have been removed. In their place are six large round tables with padded chairs. At each table stacks of poker chips and decks of cards are piled in front of a croupier in a white shirt, arm garters, and a black vest.

Six players are in their places in the chairs around each table. Gambling men are dressed in dark suits, brocade vests. Women at the tables are wearing flowered formal dresses and expensive jewelry.

A large red rope stretches from pillar to pillar around the six tables, keeping spectators from pressing too close.

Deputies guard all the windows and doors.

Flynn's guards sit on chairs around the mezzanine overlooking the six tables. Each man carries a rifle.

Patrons flood the bar, and the bartenders scramble to keep up with drink requests.

Flynn stands on the first step of the staircase in a dove grey suit with watch chain draped between his vest pockets. Beside him stands Evangeline in a pale blue long dress that conforms to her body, defining all her curves.

"This looks like an intense setting." Isaac continues to stare in awe.

"Folks are here to play serious poker, that's for sure. It took five thousand dollars per person to have a seat at one of the tables. That means Flynn has to have upwards of two hundred thousand dollars in his safe."

"What do you mean serious poker?"

"I mean once this game begins, it continues until only one person walks away the winner. Each table will be played out, gamers will move to another table, and it will play out until only one person wins."

"They win all two hundred thousand?" Isaac's voice rings with incredulity.

"Oh, hell no. Flynn ain't about to give all the money away. I heard he's got a sixty-forty split agreed to by the players. The winner takes one hundred and eight thousand and Flynn keeps seventy-two thousand."

"I cannot imagine that much money."

"Flynn can and does. Why is Evangeline hugging so close to him?"

"Like you said, Chad...greed, lust, and power. It appears Flynn has all three working for him."

"You keep learnin', Isaac, and you're bound to be plumb dangerous one of these days. Let's find the Sheriff, and then I need to tell Miss Evangeline about Naomi."

Chad weaves his way through the crowd inside the gambling hall with Isaac right behind.

Rafe and Victor move like around the base of the race track grandstands. The pungent smell of kerosene floats on the air. They continue to splash coal oil on the wooden structure. They've already saturated the walls of the club house. A lone watchman stops his buggy, smells the air, and steps down. He pulls his shotgun from the floor and turns toward the grandstands.

"Y'all come out from under them stands. I got my gun on you, so move real slow like."

Rafe walks out with his hands in the air.

"Don't shoot. My hands are up."

"What y'all doin' with coal oil under there?"

"What coal oil?"

"You dad-blamed fool, it reeks of coal oil out here. What are you doin'? Only thing that you might be doin'…oh, no. You're fixin' to burn it down, ain't you?"

"You're too smart for your own good."

Victor slips quietly behind the guard, throws one arm around his chest, and with the other yanks the Bowie knife across the man's throat. In a gurgling gasp, the guard falls to the ground. Victor wipes his knife off on the man's shirt.

"He no has to worry about the smell, no?"

"Forget him. Light the torch and set the club house on fire. I'll light up the grandstand and stables. Once they're caught and burnin' real good, we head for town. The dynamite on my horse is more than enough to do the job on Flynn's safe."

Victor strikes a match and ignites his torch. He uses it to

light Rafe's. Both men move toward the wooden structures. As they touch the coal oil, it bursts into flames that roll across the buildings, quickly turning them into fiery infernos.

The sounds that rend the night are wood snapping as it crackles and pops, consumed by the fire, and the wild high-pitched screams of terrified horses trapped in the blazing stables.

Rafe and Victor mount and race toward town.

Chad meets the Sheriff as he enters Flynn's casino.

"Saw the body out front and heard from my deputies about the attempted stabbing. You got anything else to add?"

"It was self-defense Sheriff. Naomi tried to stab Isaac and then turned on me."

"That's what my men said as well. The undertaker is hauling the body away right now. This is shaping up to be some wing-ding, ain't it?" The Sheriff looks around the gambling hall.

"It's a right big deal, that's for sure," answers Chad. "I was on my way to tell Miss Evangeline about her friend."

"Don't worry about that. I'll tell her and explain the situation. Better from me than you."

"It's your town, Sheriff. I'll wait over there by the front door."

"You do that. Stay close." The sheriff walks toward the staircase where Flynn stands with Evangeline.

17

FLYNN'S

C HAD WATCHES THE SPECTATORS PRESS AGAINST THE red rope separating the high stakes poker players in the gambling hall. Flynn's men continue to push back anyone attempting to move past the ropes. The croupiers shuffle, deal, and re-deal as cards are called for and wagers are placed. Poker chip stacks rise and fall before players as each hand is concluded. After two hours of play, a halt is called. Players stand and stretch to unkink muscles. Waiters circulate to deliver and refresh drinks. After fifteen minutes, play is resumed. Flynn walks from table to table, observing the card play. Evangeline stands close by dabbing her eyes with an embroidered handkerchief.

Chad leans close to Isaac. "Looks like she's dealin' with the news of Naomi."

"It did not take the Sheriff long to deliver the solemn message."

"I'm sure he's done it enough before," says Chad. "There's a pile of money movin' back and forth across those tables."

"There certainly is. I do not know if I would have the constitution to sit as quietly and stoically as these players knowing the next hand could wipe out a fortune."

"That's why they're playin' and you're not."

"Well, that, and the five-thousand-dollars buy-in."

"Yeah. That too."

Outside the hall, the volume of talking and shouting increases. Chad picks up on a tone of panic. Suddenly, screaming punctures the night as the crowd inside the hall surges toward the windows.

"Over there, do you see it?" A bespectacled man wearing a top hat points out the window.

"Yes, yes, it's over there." The woman beside the man points as well.

"What is it?" Another spectator questions.

"A glow, bright glow in the sky."

"No. It's a fire."

"What's burning out there?"

"Ain't nothing but forest. Is it a forest fire?"

A man shoves past Flynn's door guards into the hall. "It's on fire, Mr. Flynn."

"What's on fire? Speak up, man. What's got everybody's attention?" Flynn moves rapidly toward the man.

"Your race track."

"What?"

"Your race track, Mr. Flynn. Everything is goin' up in a blaze."

"Get out of the way, clear a path, move, move." Flynn shoves his guards into the crowd to move people aside. He steps through the doorway and looks toward the west end of Hot Springs valley. He sees a flickering orange-reddish color on the horizon and flames leaping skyward.

"Don't just stand here, get down there. Get the bucket brigade and fire engine down there now. Move, damn you, move, I can't lose that property. There are race horses in the stables. Get going, stop standing around looking, everybody move." Flynn's shouts are hysterical as he shoves the mayor and sheriff down the steps demanding immediate action.

Flynn watches the dissipating crowd that moves toward the west end of town. Buggies and carriages load up men as they move toward the race track. A clanging bell on main street signals that the horse drawn fire engine is racing toward the fire. It speeds past the gambling hall. People are running and walking rapidly in the direction of the fire.

He waves his arms at his guards.

"Get down there now. Don't stand around. Put out that fire."

The guards on the mezzanine rush downstairs and out the door. Those surrounding the poker players run after them. The two remain guards move toward the door to watch what is happening outside.

In his panic, Flynn looks around and motions to the waiters and bartenders. "Don't just stand there, get out of here and go put out that fire."

They scramble from behind the bar, drop their serving trays, and run out the front door heading for the fire.

The croupiers nervously look around. The players haven't stopped their poker games. The stakes are raised, checked, and cards called for as the unsteady hands of the dealers distribute the cards. The gamblers focus on their games and shut out everything going on around them.

Evangeline realizes this is the opportunity she's needed. She moves up behind Flynn who's come back into the hall and paces in front of the staircase.

Pulling a pepperbox derringer from her handbag, she leans close to Flynn.

"How's it feel to see everything going up in smoke, Frank?" Evangeline shoves the derringer against Flynn's back. "One false move, one wiggle for help, and I'll cut your backbone in two with this pepperbox."

"You? You did this? Why?"

"Why did you leave me beaten and robbed in St. Louis?"

"Evangeline, that was years ago."

"Seems like only yesterday to me. How's it feel to you, now?"

Flynn looks rapidly around the room for help. The poker players continue playing. His guards, waiters, and bartenders are gone. There's no one to help him.

"What do you want, Evangeline?"

Laughing a quiet hysterical laugh, Evangeline shoves the gun harder against Flynn's back. "I want you to feel what I felt when you abandoned me. Beaten, broke, and defeated."

"You've carried this hatred to this point? You've got to destroy me? Is that the picture?"

"Destroying you beyond recovery is what I've lived for since St. Louis. In order to survive, I had to kill men who owed me money for others to pay up."

"You killed men?"

"Naomi helped. She's was very effective."

"That Indian witch was always in the way."

"Shut up. She's was my friend and without her I'd never have recovered."

"You know, I only robbed you because you were planning to do the same to me."

"I've got the gun, Frank, and we're talking about you, not me. What I intended to do or not do is not the issue. What I'm doing now is settling the score. Move toward the back door, slowly. We are going to take your buggy to the train depot."

"What are you talking about?"

"Frank, I'm not stupid. I know you keep your buggy tied out back. You've never left yourself without a quick way out of any situation. Now, move. I won't ask again."

With Evangeline's prodding, Flynn walks toward the back door of the gambling hall. They see people have drifted away from the gambling hall toward the fire. Only the poker players and croupiers continue their games. The two remaining guards are on the front porch watching the fire.

"Why are you going to the train depot?" Flynn opens the back door and steps into the alley.

"The night train leaves in one hour, and we're on it." Evangeline shoves Flynn against the buggy. "Step in. Do it now."

Flynn steps into the buggy and starts to use his foot to kick Evangeline.

Evangeline swings a twelve-inch-long lead-filled black jack

crashing it against Flynn's head. He slumps onto the seat.

She unties the horse, climbs into the buggy, shoves Flynn into the corner of the seat, snaps the reins, and drives down the alley. At the corner, she stops as Rafe and Victor gallop up to her.

"The place is burning like a cold morning's fireplace. Ain't nobody goin' to put that blaze out." Rafe pulls his horse close to the buggy.

"*Si, senorita*. It burns real nice." Victor smiles his reptilian grin.

Evangeline shudders looking at him. "You've got less than one hour to blow the safe, clean it out, and meet me at the depot. You've got to finish the job with Flynn."

"Guards? Sheriff? Anybody inside to stop us?"

"Nobody, if you go now. Get the money and get to the depot. The train is the fastest way out of Hot Springs. The night train pulls out in fifty minutes. They can't catch us on it. On horseback they'll round you up before morning."

"All right, all right. We'll see you at the depot."

Evangeline yanks the reins on the buggy horse and snaps them over its back as she races for the train depot on the east end of the valley.

Rafe and Victor dismount, tie their horses to a post, and run into the gambling hall, carrying the bag of dynamite, blasting caps, and safety fuse.

The first outcry from the crowd outside the gambling hall had

Chad moving through the crowd toward the doorway. When the panic breaks out, he is on the porch looking at the fire on the west end of the valley. Isaac snakes his way through the throng of people to stand beside him.

"The race track. It has to be. Nothin' else out there to burn like that," says Chad.

"Do you think Flynn is destroying his own race track? Why would he build it only to burn it down?" Isaac watches the leaping flames mesmerized by the sight.

"Not likely. Only one person I can think of who wants to see him lose it."

"You mean Evangeline? Wait. She's inside. I saw her standing beside Flynn on the staircase." Isaac turns around trying to see inside the gambling hall.

"What better place to be than beside Flynn. Where's her brother?"

"The kerosene." A look of sudden realization floods Isaac's face as he looks at Chad.

"Yep, and Rafe Dolin to do the deed."

"Let's get back inside to question her." Chad moves toward the gambling hall entrance.

The two guards stop Chad and Isaac at the doorway.

"Step back boys," Chad orders. "Y'all got enough on your hands right now. You don't want to mix it up with two U.S. Marshals, do you?"

The two guards look at each other and step aside.

"Thank you, men. You've made a wise choice." Chad and Isaac hurry into the gambling hall.

The only sound they hear is the clatter of poker chips and the gambler's muted requests for cards. A strange eeriness settles upon the hall. The cacophony of noise is gone. Only the gamblers are creating any sounds.

Chad looks for Flynn and Evangeline.

"Do you see Flynn?" Isaac moves around Chad for a better view of the vacated hall.

"Not here. Let's go check the office." Chad walks toward the office door beside the bar.

"You don't suppose he just left, do you?"

"Not likely, Isaac. The fire, the poker game, and the money in his safe should have him rooted here."

"Why would he hide?"

"May not be hidin'. May be fixin' to run."

"You mean, steal the money and leave town?"

"I don't mean steal the money and stay. Check your pistol."

Chad pulls his Colt, flips open the loading gate, fishes a .45 cartridge from his holster belt, drops the bullet into the one empty chamber, snaps the gate closed, and spins the cylinder to make certain its ready.

At the office door, he grabs the handle and eases it open. His pistol barrel pokes through the opening.

Rafe kneels down beside the safe in Flynn's office. It sits in the corner and is four feet tall by three feet deep and wide. The front door has a tumbler and lever handle. Across the top of the door is the name Wells Fargo.

"Hurry up, *amigo*. It's no good to stick around here for long." Victor paces the office floor.

"Got to tie this dynamite to the handle, stick the cap on,

and plug it with the fuse. I'm cutting the fuse for two minutes. Once I light it, get out the back door. When the explosion springs the safe open, we can grab the money. Here goes." Rafe strikes a match and touches the safety fuse. The gunpowder laced fuse sputters and pops when lit, then flares. "Now, go."

Victor turns to rush out when he sees the office door open and a pistol barrel fill the gap.

"Get out, *amigo*." Victor shoves Rafe toward the back door as he pulls his revolver.

Rafe falls onto the door, grabs the handle, yanks it open, and bolts into the alley.

Victor pulls his pistol and triggers two quick shots toward the door before his head snaps back.

Two black holes appear in his forehead. He collapses into a pile on the floor.

The fuse burns down to the dynamite.

Chad flinches as splinters explode from the doorframe. Shoving the door open, he steps into the office prepared to shoot again.

"You killed him." Isaac steps around Chad, staring at Victor's body on the floor.

"I believe he's as dead as he's ever gonna be." Chad leans over Victor and glances up at the safe. "Get out, Isaac. The safe's gonna blow. Get out now." He rushes toward the office door.

Isaac looks at the safe, calmly walks toward it, reaches out, and pulls the sparking fuse from the dynamite. He throws it on the floor and smashes it with his boot.

"Were you worried about this?" Isaac points at the black smudge on the floor.

Leaning on the doorframe, Chad looks over his shoulder.

"What did you do?"

"Elementary my dear Chadbourne. No fuse. No explosion. It is very simple."

With his back against the wall, Chad looks at Isaac and the safe.

"So, you just pulled the fuse?"

"Certainly."

"You are one gutsy pharmacist, Isaac." Chad takes his hat off, wipes his brow, and puts it back on. "Where's Rafe?"

"The backdoor is open. I assume the rascal escaped through it."

"Let's go. He can't be far. Oh, don't step through the door. Wait until I take a look."

"As you wish, Chadbourne." Isaac steps aside, letting Chad go to the open door and survey the alley.

A pistol slug smashes into the doorframe above Chad's head. Immediately, he yanks his head back inside and leans against the wall.

"I'm gettin' real tired of folks trying to shoot me tonight."

"Would you like me to take your place?" Isaac moves toward Chad.

"No. I don't want you to take my place. Stand there until I get outside, and then come on quick-like."

"As you wish."

Chad lunges through the open doorway into the alley, rushes toward Rafe and Victor's horses, and comes to a sudden halt.

Nothing.

The alley is quiet.

"Grab that dynamite from the safe and get out here." Chad shouts to Isaac.

Quickly, Isaac appears in the doorway, dynamite in hand. Chad motions him toward the horses.

The night train blows its whistle, indicating its imminent departure. It blows a second time.

Chad looks at Isaac. A look of instant realization is on his face.

"What is it, Chad? What are you thinking?"

"It's the train, Isaac. The train."

"Certainly, it is a train. I heard the whistle."

"No. Evangeline is on the train."

"What? How do you know?"

"I just know that if I was lookin' to get out of town quick, I'd take the train."

"Why is she getting out of town?"

"Just trust me. We've got to get to the depot."

"What about Rafe Dolin?"

"Got a bigger fish to fry right now before it's too late."

Chad unties Victor's horse, mounts, and yanks the horse's head around. He spurs into a gallop. Isaac rushes to Rafe's horse, climbs into the saddle, and races after him.

Rafe runs along the sidewalk, dodging into shadows and keeping out of sight as he runs toward the depot. Two riders coming up Main Street cause him to hide in the shadow of a building. They rush past.

It's those damned marshals on my horse. They're tryin' to get to the depot. Got to get there to help Evangeline.

He runs as fast as he's able.

18

DEPOT

EVANGELINE DRIVES THE BUGGY TO THE TRAIN station and stops beside the steps leading onto the depot platform. Leaning over, she repeatedly slaps Flynn's face. His head flops from side to side until he rouses.

"Whaaat…stop. Stop. I'm awake." Groggily, Flynn sits up straighter. "I'm awake."

"Get out and up the steps." Evangeline shoves the derringer into Flynn's belly. "One false move and you're a dead man."

She slides out of the buggy, and Flynn eases over to step out onto the ground. He looks around, hoping to see someone who might save him from his dilemma.

"Nobody is here to help you. Move up the steps, onto the platform, and head for the livestock car." Evangeline moves behind Flynn, keeping the gun jammed into his back.

On the platform, they walk between stacks of crates and barrels toward the stock car. When they arrive, they step through the open door onto a straw covered floor.

Evangeline shoves Flynn from behind, sending him sprawling headlong into an open stall. He lands spread eagle on his face.

"Lie still. Don't move."

"I'm not moving. Can't we work something out. I've got money. It's yours."

"I've got what I want, Frank. I've got you, and you're being destroyed piece by piece. No reputation. No money. No life, just like you left me. Remember?"

"It was a long time ago, Evangeline. Can't we start over?"

A hysterical laugh slips from Evangeline's mouth. "Start over? With you? Never happen."

She's been listening for the dynamite's blast that has not yet happened, but she hears riders approaching the train. "Here comes my help. Now, we'll finish dealing with you."

"Please, Evangeline. Please, let's make a deal. Anything to satisfy you." Flynn squirms on the floor.

"I'm working on that, Frank. I'll be satisfied real soon." Evangeline hears footsteps approaching the stock car. "Real soon, Frank."

Chad and Isaac stop beside the buggy at the depot platform. Quietly they climb the steps and listen.

"Over there." Chad points toward the stock car. "I hear

talking over there."

"How can you hear anything over the steam being released by the engine?"

"I just do, that's all. Let's move that way."

"It's dark enough out here that seeing anything is difficult."

"Stay behind me. Come on."

Chad walks steadily toward the stock car. The voices become louder and recognizable.

"It's Evangeline and sounds like Flynn." Chad stops.

Isaac stands beside him and whispers. "What do we do now?"

"Let's go introduce ourselves."

"After you, Marshal Westerman. I'm right behind you."

Stepping from a stack of crates, Chad makes out the shape of Evangeline in the dim light from lanterns suspended along the depot platform. She's just inside the doorway of the stock car. On the floor before her lies the figure of a man he takes to be Flynn.

"Miss Evangeline, what's going on?" Chad calls.

Turning around, Evangeline's face is flooded with a look of shock and amazement.

"You. What are you doing here?" She raises her derringer toward Chad.

Flynn uses Chad's interruption to leap from the ground to a squatting position and stick out his leg. He trips Evangeline from behind.

She staggers backward.

Her arms flail around trying to grab anything for support.

The derringer goes flying through the air.

She crashes against the wall of an adjoining stall in the stock car.

"Get up real slow-like, Flynn." Chad holds his pistol steady in his hand.

"I'm the injured party here, Marshal. That maniac kidnapped me. Arrest her." Flynn points at Evangeline.

Chad looks toward Evangeline and notices blotches staining the front of her dress bodice. He sees four steel points protruding from her chest.

Stepping into the car, he quickly hurries to Evangeline and sees she is impaled on a pitchfork stuck between the slats of the stall wall.

"Miss Evangeline, stay still. I'll try to get help. Don't move."

"Too late, Marshal. Kill him for me. Shoot him down like the dog he is. He's managed to kill me again." Evangeline shifts her eyes toward Flynn. "Kill him now. For me." Blood trickles from Evangeline's mouth and drips off her chin.

"Don't talk, Miss Evangeline. We'll get help. Isaac, grab that lantern over there and sit it on the barrel by the door. Light it up."

Isaac grabs the nearby lantern and shakes it, checking for kerosene. He places it on the barrel, raises the chimney, lights the wick, resets the glass chimney, and turns up the light. It floods the stock car and platform in front of the open doorway.

"She's dead, Marshal." Flynn stands beside Evangeline's body suspended against the wall.

"Get out here where I can watch you, Flynn."

Flynn steps away from Evangeline and drops to the loading platform.

"I need to find out what happened at the gambling hall and race track, Marshal. I'm leaving this mess to you."

"Slow down, feller. You're not goin' anywhere until I say so. Isaac, find something to tie up Mr. Flynn."

Isaac searches through the crates and barrels, looking for a rope or heavy cord to use to bind Flynn.

Gasping and out of breath, Rafe reaches the depot loading platform. Quickly, he scrambles up the steps, comes to a stop, and listens. He moves toward the stock car.

Hiding behind a stack of barrels, he sees Chad holding a gun on Flynn. Evangeline is nowhere around. Pulling his pistol, he steps into the light.

"Marshal, if you'd just pull that trigger it'll save me the trouble. Where's my baby sister?"

Chad is startled by the voice, but he doesn't lower his gun. He slowly turns his head toward Rafe.

"Glad you could finally join us, Mr. Dolin. I been lookin' for you for a while."

"Looks like I found you, and my gun is aimed at your gut. Tough to get gut-shot."

"Looks like that, don't it?"

"I'd just as soon kill you and then Flynn. It don't make me no never mind. Matter-of-fact, let's just get 'er done." Rafe raises his pistol, tightening his trigger finger.

Suddenly, a sputtering sound overhead attracts everyone's attention. A stick of dynamite explodes with a powerful blast sending a shower of sparks and a concussion of force slamming down on the men on the platform.

Rafe sprawls on the platform his gun knocked from his hand.

Chad is driven to his knees with both hands clasped over his ears. His gun lies at his feet. Flynn lies on his face with his hands covering his head.

Isaac steps from behind a tarp covered pile of merchandise, his pistol leveled at Rafe.

"Mr. Dolin and Mr. Flynn, kindly stay on the ground. I would distinctly dislike having to shoot either or both of you but will not hesitate if you do not comply."

Rafe looks for a way to escape. He twitches as if to make a dash. Isaac cocks the hammer on his Colt.

"You will not make the first step, sir. I can assure you, at this range I will blow a hole through you big enough to see daylight through. On your knees, sir. Now."

Rafe crawls to his knees glaring at Isaac.

Chad motions Flynn over beside Rafe. "On your knees, Mr. Flynn. Y'all keep each other company."

Chad glances at Isaac as he retrieves his pistol and stands. "That dynamite came in handy. You could have just shot him, you know."

"That was a possibility, but I thought the dynamite was a better touch. Besides, you know how much I dislike shooting anyone." Isaac smiles.

"You've got the badge. That makes it different. Besides, my ears are still ringing." Chad slowly shakes his head.

"You and I know how upset I still am over being manipulated into taking the badge. However, I am sorry to cause you discomfort."

"Well, could you swallow your bein' upset long enough to go tell the station agent about Evangeline? I'll hold these fellers here until you get back and then we can walk them down to the jail, Marshal Wisenheimer."

"As you wish, Marshal Westerman. I will return shortly."
Isaac turns and walks to the depot office.

Flynn looks at Chad.

"Marshal, I'm a changed man. This happening has made
a profound impact on me. I'm repenting of my past ways. If
you'd see fit to let me go. I'll lead a new life."

Rafe watches Flynn and joins in.

"You know that I can change too, Marshal. I've been used
by others and now I want to repent of my ways."

Chad looks at both men's pleading faces barely able to keep
from bursting out laughing. Putting a solemn look on his face
he says, "Do y'all think I'm that soft in the head. After all, if
repentance is what y'all are seekin', it ain't mine to give except at
the end of a gun. So, you can make a break for it if you're truly
repentant." Chad pauses.

Nobody moves.

"Maybe y'all can save your pleas for Judge Parker. Now,
if you'll both lie on your bellies we'll wait for Marshal
Wisenheimer to return." Chad motions to Rafe and Flynn.

Reluctantly, they flop onto their stomachs.

19

TEXAS BOUND

THE COURT CLERKS SCURRY AROUND CHAD AND ISAAC as they sit in chairs outside Judge Parker's office in Fort Smith. Both Rafe Dolin and Frank Flynn are delivered to the 'Hell on the Border' jail in the basement of the courthouse.

Suddenly, Judge Isaac Parker yanks the door of his office open and stands in the doorway.

"What are you two waiting for, an engraved invitation? Get in here." Parker turns and stomps into his office.

Isaac looks at Chad. They shrug, get to their feet, and follow the Judge.

Taking a seat in the leather chair behind his desk, Parker looks at the marshals.

"It took you long enough to run Dolin to ground. Hell,

Bass Reeves could have been back here in two weeks with the job completed. You've been lollygagging in Hot Springs, got the town damn near burned down from what I hear, and got a leading citizen killed. What have you got to say for yourselves?"

Isaac and Chad sit taken aback by Parker's assault. Before they answer, the Judge starts again.

"I've got extradition orders for Flynn. The law in St. Louis has been looking for him for a while, and you've delivered him up for them. Dolin's going to trial next week. I imagine with the evidence we have against him, he'll hang. No slick lawyer is going to talk him off the gallows. It appears you've completed your assignment. Speak up, what have you got to say?"

"Well, Judge, it appears that we've done what we came to do. I think we need to be getting' back to Texas." Chad leans forward in the chair while speaking.

"I see. You think you need to get back to Texas." Parker looks at Isaac. "What do you think?"

"I think I don't want to be a marshal any longer, sir." Isaac looks at the floor after speaking.

"You don't want to be a marshal?"

"I would truly prefer to not be one, sir." Isaac holds his hat in his hands.

Parker rises from his chair and moves to the windows. With his hands clasped behind his back, he pats one into the other. He pauses, turns, and faces Chad and Isaac.

"I asked you men to deal with a Texas outlaw. You did. You also brought in another wanted felon. Westerman, you were on loan to me. I agree, it's time you got back to Texas." Parker moves to the office door, stops, and opens the door, allowing the pair of Marshalls to step through.

"Now, get out of my jurisdiction. Oh, you, give me back my badge." Parker points at Isaac. "I deputized you to assist. Now that the job is complete, you're no longer a marshal."

Isaac fumbles around in his jacket pocket, pulls out the badge, and hands it to Parker. "Thank you, Your Honor." Isaac puts his hat on.

"There is an afternoon train from Fort Smith that will take you to Texarkana. Be on it. I catch you two in my jurisdiction again without me sending for you, there'll be hell to pay. Do I make myself clear?"

Chad places his hat on his head.

"Thank you, Judge. It's been a pleasure. Look us up whenever you're down Texas way." Nudging Isaac, he turns to walk away.

"Just a minute. There is reward money on both Dolin and Flynn. I've already signed the paperwork. Pick it up from the clerk downstairs on your way out. Now, get out of here. I've got work to do."

Both Chad and Isaac nod and leave the office.

The chief court clerk rushes up to Judge Parker.

"Here is the court agenda for today, Your Honor." He holds out a document.

Judge Parker stands in the doorway with his thumbs hooked over his vest pockets watching Chad and Isaac depart. "There go two good U.S. Deputy Marshals. Yes, sir. Two good ones," Parker mutters to himself.

Realizing the chief clerk spoke to him, he says, "What, what did you say?" He sees the document. "Get away from me, I'll let you know what I want to do, and when."

He shoves the door closed.

AFTERWORD

I hope you enjoyed this novella. If you did, I would be very grateful if you would write a customer review. Independent Authors don't have the resources of the publishing houses. We rely on our readers to promote our books by posting reviews.

Please locate the book on Amazon.com. Type my name in the search bar. My books should appear. Click on the book title. Near the bottom of the page, just below the "More About the Author" section, you will see a Customer Review area. Please click the 'Write a customer review' button and provide your feedback on the book. It will be greatly appreciated.

William A. Burgdorf

For more information about William Burgdorf and his books, you may want to visit the author's websites:

www.waburgdorf.com,

and email: DrBilly@waburgdorf.com.

NEW RELEASE

BARBED WIRE

BY

WM. A. BURGDORF

1

AT THE WIRE

STARS FILL THE SKY. OVERHEAD THE INKY BLACKNESS is punctured by thousands of twinkling heavenly bodies. Deputy U.S. Marshal Chadbourne Westerman sits quietly in his buggy in a grove of trees watching shooting stars streak across the firmament. He wears a three-piece brown suit, well-worn boots, a collarless white shirt, and a round crown wide-brimmed Stetson hat.

The deafening silence of the night is suddenly shattered with the screams, shouts, and the thunder of hooves.

Another nightrider gang fence cutting tonight. Almost half the counties in Texas are calling for assistance and the governor requested us marshals to intervene to end the depredations of wire cutting. I've got to get to the bottom of it here in Kimble County, Texas. It sure seemed easier when I was a range detective in the hill country and on the Chisholm Trail than this. Isaac often asks me why I switched jobs and became a Deputy U.S. Marshall. Tonight, I'm thinkin' that's a fair question. Here he sits beside me, sleeping without a care in the world. It's been almost twelve years since we met on a cattle drive. Yes sir, Isaac Wisenheimer, pharmacist extraordinaire. Claims to have trained with the best back East and out here resorts to selling patent medicines. I kid him about being a snake oil peddler, and he'll never admit to it. Think I'll hang onto him a while longer as my partner.

Chad snaps the reins over the buggy horse and pulls onto the road moving quickly toward the rapidly disappearing sound of hard riding men. In the distance, a single gunshot echoes in the predawn. He snaps the reins again and the horse breaks into a trot.

Light is beginning to tinge the edges of the horizon. Isaac stirs, groans, and shifts on the buggy seat.

"You could avoid the pot holes, Chadbourne."

"No fun in that, Isaac. Besides a big enough one should bounce you off the seat."

"Was that a gunshot I heard?"

"Yep, we're heading that direction."

"I do not hear additional gunfire."

"Strange, I agree."

The morning sun leaps over the horizon and illuminates a landscape of rolling hills and grasslands. Barbed wire fencing stretches into the distance and is cut in numerous places. The wire crossing the road is cut multiple times and lies on the ground in pieces. From the trees and brush in the valleys, morning birds sing loud and long filling the air with their ode to morning.

Chad stops the buggy beside a still form lying in the roadway.

Jake Spilling lies face up in the dirt as dead as he ever will be. A single bullet hole is in the middle of his chest.

Sitting in his buggy, Chad looks at the body sprawled on the ground. Isaac Wiseinheimer leans over to glimpse at the corpse.

The man is dressed in canvas pants, boots, a blue striped shirt, a leather vest, and wears kid gloves. A floppy felt hat lies beside him.

"It does appear he was the recipient of a gunshot." Isaac studies the body.

"Yep, I reckon so."

"What is he clutching in his hand?"

"Looks like a pair of wire cutters."

"So, have we caught our fence cutter?"

"Would lead you to think that, wouldn't it?"

"You do not think it is what it appears to be?"

"I think it is just way too easy to pin it on a dead man." Chadbourne pushes his hat back on his head.

Isaac settles himself back on the buggy seat. "We have been out here for a month chasing one group of riders after another with no success. Now, at least, we have a body. That should make you happy." He straightens his blue suit coat and re-creases his trousers with his fingers. His bowler hat sits on his head at a jaunty angle. Glancing up, he looks across the open landscape of rolling hills and copse of live oaks and cottonwoods broken only by barbed wire fencing.

"Yep. We've been led on a merry chase or two. But why kill now? After all the chases with no deaths, why kill now?" Chad leans forward for a better view of the body.

"I do not follow you. What do you mean, *why now*?" asks Isaac.

"I mean, there have been more than ample opportunities to kill before. I'm sure many more than we know about. Now, they start killing. It doesn't make good sense."

"When does killing ever make good sense? You are looking for answers that just are not there."

"Maybe, but this leaves a big hole in my picture of what's goin' on." Chad steps from the buggy to investigate the dead man. He searches the pockets of the deceased for anything that remains on the body. "You do recognize him, right?"

"Oh, yes. It is Jake Spilling. I've seen him often enough at the Dry Well Saloon in Junction City." Isaac leans over to confirm his statement. "He has a missus and two underfed children on a hardscrabble farm."

"Didn't ever appear he was working hard enough to make anything out of that farm either."

"Does this mean the fence cutting has been dealt with permanently?"

"If you accept that Jake is guilty. I've never known him to willingly do anything that might put him in harm's way. He's a lingerer, a loafer, and this doesn't fit my picture of him." Chad shoves his hat further back on his head.

"So, we stay put? Not going back to Austin?"

"That's the drift. We stay put. The governor wants this problem to go away, and one questionable cowboy with clippers in his hand and lying dead doesn't tie everything up in a package with ribbons."

"Sometimes, you can be exasperating. You know that?" Isaac removes his bowler, takes a monogramed handkerchief from his coat, wipes the hatband, puts his hat back on, and carefully folds the handkerchief before placing it back into his pocket.

"Yep. Give me a hand loading him on the back of the buggy. We'll take him to the undertaker in town."

"I am a pharmacist, not a mortician."

"You're my partner, so grab a hold."

"Where?"

"Well, if I've got his hands, where do you think you should grab a hold?"

"His feet, obviously, but do you know what his boots have been through?"

"No, Isaac. I don't. But he ain't gonna jump up and climb on the wagon by himself. So, grab a hold."

"Very well. I do not like it, but I will do it."

Stepping from the buggy, Isaac grabs the tops of the corpse's boots while Chad holds his arms. Together, they swing the body and toss it up onto the baggage rack of the buggy. Both climb back aboard.

"This is a fine kettle of fish. Here I am, a board-trained pharmacist who learned from the best in the profession back east, loading a corpse on a wagon."

"You were selling snake-oil patent medicine when I found you."

"I was providing relief and comfort for those unfortunates snared in malady's firm embrace."

"You were selling spiked whiskey as Dr. Wiseinheimer's Elixirs."

"Why quibble over incidentals?" Isaac dismisses the argument with a wave of his hand. "It is still most undesirable to wrestle with a corpse."

"It ain't top on my list either, but it's gotta be done."

Chad snaps the reins over the horse's back, and they head for town.

Holding his hat in his hands, a tall, lean, blonde-haired cowboy stands in the massive stone and timber-built ranch headquarters home beside a huge central fireplace. He fidgets with his hat while waiting for the large man seated at the desk with salt-and-pepper hair, greying beard, and mustache to speak. The man slowly chews an unlit cigar passing it frequently from one side of his mouth to the other. Yanking the stogie from his mouth, he hurls it toward the fireplace.

"You know I didn't want to call any attention to the fence cutting night riders, right?"

"Yes, Mister Armitage, I know that." The cowboy continues to nervously twist and turn the hat in his hands.

"Yet, you're standing here telling me that someone was killed?" Armitage slams a beefy hand down on the desktop. The cowboy flinches at the sound.

"Yes, sir. It was an accident."

"Accident. Hell, killing someone is no accident. You know that Governor Ireland is wanting an excuse to bring Texas Rangers or army into this fracas."

"Mister Armitage, sir, we didn't kill nobody. The night riders were there at our fence when we rode up. There was gunfire. The group split up, and there was Jake Spilling on the ground."

"This ain't goin' to do us any favors. That limp-rag governor will do anything to keep trouble like fence cutting from tarnishing his administration. We've already got a Deputy U.S. Marshal sniffing around everything that's goin' on, and he's lookin' for someone to blame."

"Well, sir. That's why we left the fence cutters on Jake's body. Maybe, that'll show the Marshal we ain't the problem."

"Only if he's blind and stupid, and I don't peg that Westerman fella bein' either one of them."

"Yes, sir."

"Get out of here. I need some time to think things through." The man behind the desk stands.

"Yes, sir, Mister Armitage." The cowboy spins around and dashes from the room exiting the house.

Moving to the fireplace, the tall muscular grey-haired man picks up an andiron, places one foot on the raised hearth, and prods at smoldering oak logs on the grate.

I've spent my lifetime building this ranch, three hundred thousand acres of cattle country. With the railroad in San Antonio, I don't need to drive my herds north and suffer the losses. Only have a half-assed crew around me now to run the spread, and I ain't gonna see any pissant rancher help himself to my territory. It might be unwritten law of open range that Texas grass and water belongs to all, but Charlie Goodnight, Shanghai Pierce, and 'Bigfoot' Wallace see fit to use barbed wire to protect water and grazing rights for their herds and I aim to do the same. I can't help it this drought is hanging on, and the small open range idiots in Kimble County can't see the writing on the wall. If my boys were here, they'd make sure our herds are protected, but they're dead, killed by Comanche and Kiowas. Louis Armitage viciously stabs the logs in the fireplace and returns the andiron to its rack. He turns and leaves the room.

"That's it sheriff. Spilling was lying dead as a door nail when we found him." Chad has one foot propped up on the front edge of the desk pushing his chair back into a reclining position.

"Not surprised at Spilling bein' dead. But, a wire cutter? That just ain't in the boy." The sheriff shakes his bald head while his hands busily reload the pipe he picks up from his desk. Brushing excess tobacco from the blotter and off his pants, he pulls a match from his vest pocket, and lights his pipe. Taking a deep drag, he blows smoke rings toward the ceiling. "Nope, just not in Jake to cut wire."

"That's my take as well, sheriff. Who would put him up to doing something like that?" Chad shifts in his chair and rebalances himself.

"My guess is that he might be night riding with the Owls, Javelinas, or Blue Devils as some of the marauders call themselves."

"Fancy names for criminal activities," says Chad.

"They ain't all criminals. A bunch are open range ranchers who are terrified by the thought of barbed wire takin' away water and graze from their herds. With the drought, who can blame them? Some are drifters who'll find trouble, and a few are gun sharps aimin' for trouble."

"I can understand the ranchers. That's for certain."

"Especially when some large ranchers enclose public lands within their own spread. Some even fence off small ranches legally owned by other persons. Public roads are blocked off, keepin' folks from schools, churches, and even from delivering the mail. Look here." The sheriff stands, moves to a framed county map on the wall, and points at different locations. "Here, here, and here the barbed wire is strung across the roads. I've talked with the ranchers about opening up the right of way, but nothing is being done."

"Sounds like things are goin' from bad to worse, sheriff." Chad drops his foot to the floor and sits upright in the chair.

"That ain't the half. With this drought hangin' on like its doin', we're sittin' on a keg of blasting powder. I don't know how long I could listen to my cattle bawlin' their heads off for water without doin' something extreme."

"Even kill somebody?" asks Isaac.

The sheriff turns his head and gazes out the window for a long time.

"If I had to, I would," he answers.

ABOUT THE AUTHOR

WILLIAM BURGDORF leverages a lifetime of experiences into his stories accumulated from being born along the mighty Ohio River in southern Indiana, raised in the wide, wild desert vistas of Arizona, having lived in lake-strewn Michigan, as well as the hills and hollows of Tennessee, and now in his piney woods home in East Texas. His love of, and a double major in, history along with his successful career as an adult educator prepared him to become a masterful storyteller of historical fiction. His careful attention to exacting details, colorful and memorable characters, descriptive locales, and articulate dialogue weave together stories that engage and enthrall.

"My goal is to provide a story that captures your imagination and is remembered. At the end of the day, I desire to be regarded as a good 'storyteller.'

Website: www.waburgdorf.com
Facebook: www.facebook.com/william.burgdorf